# JOB
## A Modern Perspective

LaQuanda S. Washington

# Copyright Material

Scripture references can be found at https://www.biblegateway.com/.

Editor: Tamika Sims | Ink Pen Diva Manuscript Critique Services, LLC

Published by Kingdom Haven Publishing, LLC. kingdomhavenpublishingllc@gmail.com

ISBN: 978-0-9988913-0-9

# Acknowledgments

First and foremost, I must give all honor to God. Without Him, this book would NEVER have been possible.

*Mom:* If I lived to be a thousand years-old, it still wouldn't be long enough to thank you for all that you have sacrificed for us. I love you!

*Leah & Taj Jr.:* Everything that I am and everything that I do is for you.

*Big George, George, Kinyatta, Bobby:* Thank you for being there whenever I needed you.

*Delphia:* Thank you for seeing something in me that I didn't see in myself.

*Terri:* Thank you for forcing me outside of my comfort zone and teaching me the value of true friendship.

*Tamika:* You're my editor, encourager and motivator. Thank you for making me believe that I can do this and pushing me to think higher!

Thanks to my amazing family and friends for your unwavering love & support throughout the years.

# CHAPTER ONE

Job opened his eyes as the quiet buzzing of the cell phone alarm awakened him. He leaned over and kissed the back of his beautiful wife's neck. Job smiled as Roni gently stirred. He lightly touched her swollen belly before quietly tiptoeing out of bed.

Job knelt at the foot of their bed and began to pray. Prayer has always been an active part of Job's life and had become a part of his morning ritual. After several minutes, Job finished praying and entered the bathroom where he emerged moments later wearing his gray sweatpants and his favorite black hooded sweatshirt.

Job walked down the hallway of his large home, silently looking in on each of his children, just as he did every morning before heading out for the day's jog. Early morning sunrises were Job's favorite time of day. He jogged down the driveway, waving as he passed his security team.

Job basked in the comforting silence of being alone on the quiet stretch of road. Mornings was his God time. His philosophy has always been put God first, and everything else will fall into place. Job ran and communed with God for one hour every day before heading home to get the rest of his day started.

As he entered the kitchen after his run, Roni had just finished pouring him a cup of his favorite coffee. "Good Morning babe," Job smiled as he walked in the kitchen with sweat pouring off him.

"Hey handsome, how was your run?" she asked, handing him a towel. Job accepted the sheet and wiped the sweat dripping from his head, hugging his wife after he dried himself.

Job and Roni met 21 years ago while in college at Princeton University. Job was a popular sophomore and Roni, a shy incoming freshman. They met one chilly morning when Roni got lost looking for freshman orientation. They fell in love immediately and have been inseparable ever since. He knew from the moment he looked into her eyes that she would be his wife someday.

"It was great," Job smiled, accepting the cup of coffee she offered while softly kissing her lips. Roni was a beautiful woman. In Job's mind, her beauty had increased through the years. Her outer beauty is magnified by the fact that she has a heart of gold. Roni was one of the most giving women that Job had ever encountered.

They both have a passion for helping others. They even started a food and coat drive for low-income families in Camden, NJ while in college and were determined to instill those very same values in their children.

After taking a few sips of his coffee, Job sat the mug down on the beautiful marble island and pulled his wife close to him. "I love you so much," he whispered in her ear. "Hmmm, I love you too baby," she said as she squeezed him tightly. Job caressed her cheek as his left hand moved down to her big, beautiful belly.

Their housekeeper Anita entered the kitchen shaking her head, "Here we go again," she laughed. "You two just remember that's what led to those six sleeping angels upstairs, as well as that little one baking in your belly." Job and Roni both laughed. "Well you know seven is the number of completion," Job teased and leaned down and kissed her belly. "Job you are a mess," Anita responded as she lightly hit him with the dish towel.

As if right on cue, five-year-old Joshua, one of their twin boys, ran into the kitchen yelling, "Good morning!" "Hey little man," Job smiled as he scooped him up in his arms. "You didn't wake your brother, did you?" Job asked. "Nope, he's still sleeping. I sneaked out quietly daddy."

"Good job and you snuck out, not sneaked out," Job lovingly corrected. "Oh yeah, that's what I meant daddy," Joshua giggled, showing his newly missing tooth. Joshua leaned over and kissed his mother on the cheek, tightly hugging his father's neck.

Roni smiled as she watched them together, laughing as Job tickled Joshua. Job was such a fantastic father, and their children adored him. Roni never knew her father so she was determined to marry a man who would love and devote himself to his children. Job went above and beyond her highest expectations. Roni loved the way he interacted with each of their children. He had a unique relationship with each one of them.

Joshua, the most rambunctious of their twin boys, loves trains, so that's something he shared with his dad. They have a massive train set. Every year, the two of them attend The Great Train Expo and add another piece to their vast train collection.

Joshua's twin brother Jacob has a passion for Legos. He and Job travel to North Carolina every year to attend the Lego KidsFest. Job isn't the type of father who just wanted to spend time with his children for the sake of spending time with them. He loved creating memories with them.

Their nine-year-old James takes after his father athletically. He is a phenomenal basketball and football player and boxer. James has the athletic build of a fourteen-year-old. At nine-years-old, he's already receiving attention from several high schools. He and Job work out together daily, and Job rarely misses any of his practices or games.

Their twelve-year-old, Aaron, is interested in anything involving cars. Job recently purchased a black 1965 GTO convertible. Aaron and Job spend as much time as they can restoring the old car on the weekends. Job plans to give it to him the day he gets his driver's license. They also attend the auto show every year when it comes into town.

Angel is their only daughter and Job's pride. At 16, she's still daddy's little princess. Job had a hard time when she became interested in boys, but once a month Job and Angel have their daddy and daughter date.

He takes her to a nice restaurant, and they see a movie, concert or a play afterward. Job tries to set high standards for her so she will know how a man should treat her. At times, Roni felt that Job was spoiling her a bit too much, but he explained that he wanted to set the bar high so that Angel knew her value and would never settle for anything less.

Roni smiled thinking of their oldest son Daniel. He and Job are more like best friends than father and son. Roni couldn't believe that he would be turning 18 years-old this year. Daniel idolized his father from the time he was born and loved him more than anything.

Their passion is boating, jet-skiing and virtually anything related to water. Daniel loved the beach just as much as his father. Daniel helped Job select their family yacht, and the two of them take trips to the Chesapeake Bay and Virginia Beach areas regularly to go crabbing and fishing.

People always commented that they have such a loving family, but Roni and Job never take it for granted. They know family and friends who were dealing with significant attacks against their families and thanked God every day for their children. Job worked with a lot of troubled teens and young men. He saw firsthand what can happen when there isn't a father in the home.

He made a point of being there as often as he could for the young men he mentored. Job even started a scholarship foundation specifically for young men who have been incarcerated to help them get their lives back on track when they are released.

He had hired several of the young men he mentored to work at his investment firm over the years. In addition to giving them a job, he taught them how to properly manage their finances and budget their money so that they didn't have to live paycheck to paycheck. Roni was extremely proud of Job, and she felt so blessed to share her life with him.

She was amazed at how much Joshua and Jacob looked like their father more and more every day. Job is a handsome, tall man at 6'5". He had maintained the same athletic build that he had when they met in college. Although she had gained weight with each one of her pregnancies, Job never made her feel insecure which only made her love him more.

Roni was so caught up in her thoughts that she hadn't noticed Josh walk up to her. "Did you brush your teeth and wash your face?" she asked. "Yes ma'am and I washed the toothpaste off," Joshua answered proudly.

"Sweetie, what do you mean you washed the toothpaste off?" Roni asked. "It fell in the toilet," Joshua said with a straight face. Job burst out laughing, looking at Roni and Anita's facial expressions. Roni kissed the top of her son's head as she mouthed, "Throw it out now," to her husband.

"What's funny?" Joshua asked as he looks between the adults. "Nothing sweetie," Roni answered. "Wait, did you wash your hands after you took the toothpaste out of the toilet?" Roni asked. "The water was already clean mommy," Joshua said. Job laughed even harder as he and Roni ushered their son out of the kitchen.

"Come on little man, let's go get you washed up," Job said. As he looked over his shoulder, he saw Anita with her yellow gloves and Clorox bottle and began to laugh even harder. "God, I love my life," Job said, carrying Joshua upstairs.

Job and Roni entered their twin sons' bedroom to ensure that everything was thoroughly clean and germ-free. They were departing for vacation in a few hours and Job needed to get a few work issues resolved before he could meet his family in Hawaii.

As Job and Joshua finished up in the bathroom, Roni sat on the bed with Jacob, Joshua's twin brother. He slowly began to rouse from his sleep as she played with his hair. "Morning mommy, morning daddy, morning Joshie," Jacob said as he stretched, realizing they are all in the room.

Job walked over and hugged Jacob, "Good morning little man. You sleep okay?" Job asked with a smirk as he noticed dried drool across the entire right side of his son's face. "I slept great daddy. I had a dream about swimming," Jacob said excitedly.

That sounds like a great dream. The hotel has a huge pool with four waterslides," Job said. "Yay!" Joshua and Jacob yelled happily. "Okay, okay," Job laughed. "Your mom has already set your clothes out so go ahead and wash your face and brush your teeth and get ready. I will be back in a little while," Job said as he exited their room.

Job knocked softly on his daughter's bedroom door. "Come in," Angel said. "Good morning princess, Good morning Ashleigh," Job smiled as he kissed Angel and greeted her best friend. "Good morning Mr. A," Ashleigh smiled. "I see you both are all packed and ready to go," Job smiled. "Daddy, I cannot wait to get to Hawaii and thank you so much for letting Ashleigh come with us." "Yeah, thanks Mr. A, I've never been on a plane before," Ashleigh said.

"You're both welcome girls. It's my pleasure. We're going to have so much fun, but right now I need to get ready for work. Angel when you finish up in here would you mind helping your mom with your brothers for me, please? Breakfast will be ready in 20 minutes."

"No problem daddy," Angel smiled. "Thanks, baby-girl," Job said exiting her room and continuing down the hall to James and Aaron's room. Before he reached the door, Aaron came out of the bedroom fully dressed, dragging his suitcase.

"Morning Aaron," Job said. "Morning Dad. Is breakfast ready yet? I'm starving," Aaron responds. "When aren't you hungry?" Job laughed. "You've got about 20 minutes. You all set?" "Yes sir," Aaron said. "Good, you mind helping Anita out for me? Job asked. "Sure dad," Aaron replied. "Thanks, man. Is your brother awake?" "Yes, he's getting dressed now," Aaron answered.

Job knocked on the door. "Come in dad," James said. "How did you know it was me?" Job asks as he starts shadow boxing with his son. "I heard you and Aaron talking," James responds as he side-steps a punch before hugging his father. Job grabs his son and kisses the top of his head.

"You good?" Job asked as he sat on the edge of the bed. "Yes sir," James answered. "You sure?" Job pressed. "Your mom mentioned that you have something to tell me." James who was the most talkative of the bunch is unusually quiet. "Have a seat son," Job said softly. James sat on the edge of the bed beside his father. "Now talk to me. What's up?"

James held his head down as he began to speak. "Son, look at me. You always look a man in the eye when you talk to him," Job instructed. James lifted his head as the tears that he was fighting to hold back threatened to fall down his face. "Mrs. Andrews gave out our progress reports yesterday, and my grades have dropped a little. She said if I don't pass the next three tests, my final grade for the 3rd quarter will be a D," James said through his tears.

Before Job responded, he sat back and looked at his son. James was more like him than any of his other children. "Okay, why'd your grades drop son? Last quarter you had a B, what happened?" Job asked. James looked at his father apprehensively, "I missed some of my homework assignments and failed a few class assignments." "Okay, why did you miss the assignments?" Job asked.

"I don't have an excuse dad. I was too tired after practice and didn't feel like doing them," James said. "What was our agreement?" Job asked his son. "I can't play ball if my grades drop," James responded as more tears fell. "James, I love you son and I know how much ball means to you, but your education comes first.

There are hundreds of athletes out there right now who made millions of dollars and are now broke. I won't allow you to become one of them. Your education must always come first. You don't have to stop playing forever, just until you can bring your grades back up and keep them up.

Are you having any issues or were you not doing the work?" "Just not doing the work," James sniffed. "Okay, well when we get back we'll go in and talk to your teacher together to get you back on track okay?" James nodded his head as he wiped away his tears.

He hated to disappoint his father. "I love you man," Job said hugging his son again. "I love you too dad," James responded, tightly hugging his father. "Alright, I need to hurry up and get ready to drop you guys at the airstrip."

"You all packed?" Job asked. "Yes sir, I finished packing last night," James answered, "my man," Job smiled, amazed at how much his son reminded him of himself when he was his age. "Breakfast is almost ready." "Okay, I will be down as soon as I'm finished getting dressed," James said. "Okay, don't be too long," Job said as he headed out the door.

"Morning pops," Daniel yelled from the top of the stairs. "Hey man, you all set?" Job asked. "Yes sir. My bag is already downstairs. Momma Nita asked me to come and check on everybody. She's getting ready to fix the eggs," Daniel said. "Okay, tell her to give me 15 minutes. Your mom and sister are helping your brothers and James is getting ready now." "Okay, I will let her know," Daniel said as he headed back down the stairs.

As promised, 15 minutes later, Job was walking into the dining room tying his tie. Anita placed the orange juice on the table as Job took his seat at the head of the table. They all grabbed hands as Job began to say grace.

*"Father God we ask that you bless this food which we are about to receive and bless the hands that prepared it. Allow this food to nourish our bodies and give us the*

*strength to be a blessing to someone else. In Jesus' name, we pray Amen."*

"Amen," they all say in unison as they begin to pass the food around and discuss their trip to Kauai, Hawaii. Anita had become a member of the family over the last ten years. Roni was adamant about not having some stranger in her home, but she needed help. Thankfully, as soon as Job's mother Angela introduced them, they knew Anita would be the perfect fit. Anita was a widow who lost her only son several months after losing her husband of 40 years, and she had become more of a mother to Roni than her biological mother had ever been.

After they finished breakfast, they all hugged Anita and said their goodbyes as they prepared to depart for Hawaii. Anita usually joined them on family vacations, but one of her friends from church recently had surgery and Anita had already agreed to stay with her before the scheduling of the trip.

The boys helped their father load the truck while Angel and Ashleigh get the twins settled for Roni. Job hated the thought of sending his family off without him, even for a day, but he could not miss the meeting with his board members. Roni initially suggested that they postpone the trip, but Job didn't want to disappoint the children and told her to go on without him and he'd join them the next day.

On the short drive to their private airfield, the kids discussed their vacation plans. Anthony Hamilton's '*Best of Me*' came on the radio and Job turned the volume up. "Oh yeah, that's what I'm talking about," he smiled as he glanced at his beautiful wife and began to sing to her as the kids all laughed. "Come on dad," James groaned. Daniel, Angel, and Ashleigh shook their heads before returning their attention to their smartphones. They were all extremely excited.

Job caressed Roni's hand and kissed it gently while silently counting his blessings. They were not what you'd call poor growing up, but his father wasn't a wealthy man when it came to finances. He and his siblings didn't always get everything they wanted, but they had more than what they needed. Job promised himself as a young man that he'd work hard to provide a great life for his children and that he did. They are enrolled in private schools and have traveled the world.

As they arrived at the airstrip, the kids began yelling. Roni leaned over and kissed her husband, "By the way, did I thank you for leaving me with seven overly excited kids for the next 24 hours?" Roni asked sarcastically. "I know baby," Job said, "I'm sorry, but I promise I will be there before you know it." He softly kissed her lips again.

"Ooohhh mommy and daddy kissing," Joshua snickered. "Hey, if mommy and I didn't kiss none of you would be here," Job smirked. "Kill the visual Jesus," Daniel teased, shaking his head as everyone exited the car laughing.

The crew began unloading their vehicle and Job kissed his wife once again. "Baby, I'm going to miss you so much," Job said as he pulled her close, holding her tightly. "I won't be able to sleep tonight."

"Alright, guys it's time to board," the flight attendant announced. The kids ran to get on the plane yelling and laughing. Job looked at his wife again and smiled apologetically. "It's not too late to change your mind," Job laughed. "And deal with this disappointed bunch for the rest of the day. I don't think so," Roni laughed. Job helped his wife aboard their private plane.

"Okay guys come on, so we can pray," Roni said. Job's pilot and friend, Mateo, exited the cockpit smiling as the kids run to him. Mateo and Job have known each other since high school.

Mateo wanted to be a pilot for as long as Job had known him. He worked for a popular commercial airline until they went bankrupt. Job hated airports and always wanted a private plane, so when the opportunity presented itself to help himself and his childhood friend, he couldn't resist.

"Hey, I missed you guys," Mateo said as he hugged the kids, Job, and Roni. "Roni, how is it that with each pregnancy you get even more beautiful?" Mateo asked. "Okay okay, enough of that Teo," Job laughed. "Next thing I know you'll be trying to kidnap my wife and fly her all over the world," Job joked. "Well I do love Pari," Roni laughed.

They all laughed as they gathered hands with Mateo and the crew to pray before departing. After praying, Job said his goodbyes and hugged and kissed all his children. He was overcome with emotion as he stood near the exit of the plane watching his family. He had never spent a night away from his wife or children before, and it was more emotional than he had anticipated. Roni glanced at Job and noticed the sadness on his face. She pulled him off the plane while the kids talked to the crew and buckled their seat belts.

"Baby, are you okay?" Roni asked. "Yes baby, I'm fine. I don't know what happened, I guess it's just being away from you all," Job said. "I understand baby," Roni said as she began to tear up. "By this time tomorrow, you'll be lying in my arms on the beach," Roni smiled as she rubbed her husband's head. Job nodded his head and forced a smile, not trusting himself to speak.

He helped his wife back on the plane and watched as the doors closed. He waved goodbye to his family as they excitedly waved back. Job stood back near his truck, watching as the plane took off. He watched the plane until he could no longer see it anymore. As soon as he got in the truck his cell phone rang.

"Good Morning Leslie," Job said to his sister/office manager. "I'm on my way in right now." "Job please get here as soon as possible. There are FBI agents everywhere, telling us to leave the building," Leslie panicked. "Job I think this has something to do with Samuel," Leslie said. "I'm on my way," Job sighed. Job immediately began praying. *"Lord please send your angels ahead of me and give me wisdom. Let the truth prevail and destroy every trap set by the enemy."*

# CHAPTER TWO

As soon as Job arrived, he was in complete shock. FBI agents and employees were everywhere. Job found a place to park, while a few of his employees, including Leslie, rushed over to him. Job knew at that moment that Leslie was right.

Job had fired Samuel, his friend and chief operating officer, along with the entire accounting team last week when one of the new auditors that he'd hired, who also happened to be a friend and fellow church member, found that hundreds of millions of dollars were missing from several departmental budgets and accounts including the company retirement plan and Job's charity foundation.

Job held a company meeting on Friday to inform the staff of everything that happened without going into specific details. He was preparing to meet with his lawyers, board of directors and an independent group of auditors this morning to discuss further action, but the FBI beat him to the punch. All Job could think about is his family. He needed Roni now more than ever.

"Job I heard them mention something about money. I know this has something to do with Samuel," Leslie said, looking at her twin brother with concern. "I contacted Matt already, and he should be here any moment." Job was so grateful for his sister. He'd completely forgotten to contact his lawyer. Job looked up and noticed two agents walking toward him.

"Mr. Arrington, I'm Agent Thomas Williams, and this is my partner, Agent Antonio Benavidez. We need to speak with you sir." By this time several more employees have gathered around. "Absolutely," Job responded, "It's a little chilly out here. Do my employees need to sit through this as well?" Job asked. "Yes, we will need to question all of them as well Mr. Arrington," Agent Williams said firmly. "I understand," Job conceded.

"Would it be alright if they went inside or to the hotel next door?" Job asked. "I just don't want them waiting around in the cold." "They can wait in the hotel lobby," Agent Williams reluctantly agreed. "Thank you, sir," Job sighed, relieved. "Hey guys, look I'm so sorry about all of this. The agents will need to question all of you."

"They've agreed to allow you to get out of this cold, so they are going to escort you next door to the hotel. Please grab some breakfast and relax as much as you can.

Leslie, please be sure to take care of everyone with food and anything else that they may need," Job said, trying to make the best of this situation. Leslie nodded and hugged her brother tightly wishing there was something she could say or do to make this entire mess disappear.

Job had never felt so discouraged. He fought back his tears while trying his best to hold firm to his faith. Job was a good, honorable man. None of his employees doubted his innocence for one second. Before they departed, Leslie and several other employees held hands with Job and began to pray. Agent Williams was also a man of God.

He'd seen so many of these guys come in, gain employees trust and rip them off and he assumed that Job was another opportunist. He was immediately convicted for his prejudgment. "Lord, please forgive me for judging this man," Agent Williams silently prayed. As the prayer concluded, Job was lead to the building as Leslie directed the employees to follow her to the hotel.

The lobby was essentially vacant except for a dozen or so agents milling about. As they entered the elevator Job took a deep breath. He knew that he had done nothing wrong, but he didn't want his company or his reputation to suffer because of someone else's greed.

The elevator doors opened on the floor of the executive suites, and it was a completely different scene from the lobby. Agents were everywhere yelling back and forth. Job saw several men in Samuel's office.

His knees felt weak, but he continued moving forward. As the agents escorted him to the conference room, he sat down and looked up to the Heavens pleading for help. When Job finally looked around the table his eyes fall upon a familiar face from his past. Seated three seats down was his first love, Kimberly "Kimmy" Godwin.

"Kim?" Job asked. "Hi Job," Kimberly said quietly. Job could not believe his eyes. He had not seen Kimmy since the day they left for different colleges. As much as they loved each other during that time, they both agreed that they were too young to try to deal with being away from home and a long- distance romance. Job and Kim continued to gaze at each other until Agent Williams cleared his throat.

"Would you like to call your lawyer before we speak," the agent asked. "He's on his way, but we can begin without him. I have nothing to hide." Job answered.

"Job are you sure?" Kim interjected. "You may want to talk to your lawyer before we proceed." Job smiled defeated, "Yes Kim I'm sure, but thank you."

Before Job could continue, another agent escorted his lawyers into the room. "Job I'm so sorry, we came as soon as Leslie called. Matt looks around the table. Hello, my name is Matthew McIntyre, and this is my colleague Lewis Cohen. We will be representing Mr. Arrington."

"Well then let's get started Mr. Arrington," the agent said as Matthew and Lewis took seats near Job. "Mr. Arrington, I could not help, but notice that you never asked what we were doing here," Agent Williams said, leaning back in his seat. Job pulled several documents from his portfolio including the information he e-mailed around to the staff on Friday and handed them to Agent Williams who reviewed them and passed them around.

Job rubbed his temples as his head started pounding, "Last week my new auditor discovered massive amounts of money missing from several departmental accounts. He traced the money, and it led back to my colleague Samuel Jacobson. I confronted Samuel and subsequently ended up firing the entire department. It didn't go well, and I had to have them all escorted from the building.

As you can see from the e-mails, I immediately notified my staff making sure they were aware of what we'd discovered. I'm supposed to be on my way to Hawaii with my family as we speak, but I delayed my departure to meet with an independent group of auditors and notify my board of directors today."

Everyone around the table was stunned. The agents thought Job was another swindler, but here was a man who trusted his financial team who betrayed him. It appeared that Job was doing everything he could to rectify the situation.

After several hours of reviewing the documents Job submitted, Agent Williams and several agents excuse themselves and exit the room, taking the documents with them. Job conferred with his lawyers before getting up to get a cup of coffee. Kimberly walked up behind him and lightly touched his arm, "Hi stranger," she smiled gloomily. "I'm sorry we have to meet again under these circumstances." "Me too," Job sighed.

"Look I know the truth will come out Job. The only real issue is finding out how much damage was done. That was an excellent idea for you to have your finances audited annually," Kim said. "Thanks Kimmy," Job smiled. "You look amazing." Kim blushed, "Thank you." "You should've seen my jaw drop when I realized it was your company we were investigating." "I can imagine," Job nodded. "I keep thinking about my family," Job said.

"You have such a beautiful family Job," Kim smiled. "I saw the pictures in your office. They are so adorable and those twins. I could just eat them up. I see you're aiming for your very own starting line-up," she teased. Job couldn't help but laugh. "Yes, and we have another on the way," Kimberly was genuinely excited for him. "Oh my gosh! WOW. Congratulations Job," Kim said.

"Thanks Kimmy. Last I heard you were married and pregnant," Job said. Kim looked away, "I left my husband two years ago and, I..I lost the baby," she stuttered. Job grasped Kim's hand, "Oh my gosh Kimmy, I am so sorry. I had no idea. How are you?" Job asked. Kim smiled sadly as tears that she refused to let fall welled up in her eyes. "I'm getting better every day." Job wasn't sure if it was appropriate or not to hug her in this setting, but he did it anyway. "Kimmy if you need anything at all please do not hesitate to call me." Kim nodded as the others re-entered the room with the board members and the auditors in tow.

"Mr. Arrington I'm so sorry for the delay. We just released your employees. We have their contact information should we need to question them further," Agent Williams said. "Thank you," Job said. "I know this has been pretty stressful for them as well."

After several more hours around the table it was clear to everyone else that Job was as much a victim as everyone else. However, they still had a procedure to follow. During the search for Samuel, they discovered that he departed for Oman shortly after being fired. "Mr. Arrington, it will take some time for us to see just how extensive this breach is, but we will try to complete this process as soon as possible," Agent Williams said.

"In the meantime, I'm sorry, but we have frozen your assets," the agent said. Job could believe his ears. "What??!" Job exclaimed. Agent Williams, my family, just landed in Hawaii," Job said looking at his watch. God, this cannot be happening." "Trust me, Mr. Arrington, I understand, but this is our procedure. I truly am sorry. We will work to resolve this matter as fast as possible." Job held his head down and silently prayed. "Well, look guys it's been a long day. I think we can call it quits," Agent Williams said closing the file.

Before Agent Williams finished speaking, an agent rushed into the room and passed the agent a note. Agent Williams excused himself. A short time later he reentered with a strained look on his face. "Agent Godwin, may I speak with you for a moment?" "We'll be right with you Mr. Arrington," Agent Williams said, closing the door.

Job was still trying to wrap his mind around the fact that his assets were frozen. Roni and his children were on the other side of the world with no money, and he wasn't there to look after them. He hoped that they'd be able to check into the hotel. Job could not believe that this was happening. Kim rubbed his shoulder as she walked away. "We'll get this straightened out I promise," Kim said before exiting the room.

As soon as she stepped out of the door, she could tell by the look on Thomas' face that whatever it was, it was bad, really bad. "Thomas, what is it?" Kim asked. Thomas cleared his throat. "You have a personal relationship with Mr. Arrington, right?" he asked.

"Yes, but that will not interfere with our investigation "It's not that Kim," Thomas stopped her. "The plane that was carrying his family crashed a few hours ago. There were no survivors; his wife, the seven children, the pilot, co-pilot and three crew members, all gone." Thomas looked sick to his stomach.

He was pretty sure that Mr. Arrington was innocent, but even if he were guilty, he wouldn't wish this on anyone. Thomas silently began to pray for Job's strength. He would need it now more than ever. "We need to tell him and I'm hoping you'd be up to breaking the news," Agent Williams says. "Oh my God," Kim said as she looked in the direction of the conference room. Job already appeared so broken. She staggered to a nearby chair. Kim wasn't sure how he would handle this devastating blow.

She knew this was going to be hard, but she knew that she should be the one to do it. "Are you sure?" she asked pleadingly, hoping for a different answer. "Unfortunately, yes," the older agent replied. "I will tell him," Kim cried. "Kim are you sure you're up to this?" Thomas asked. "Yes," Kim nodded. Thomas hugged her tightly. They had gotten quite close since she transferred to the Bureau headquarters. Thomas was like a father to her, and he and his wife thought of Kim as the daughter they never had. She looked over where two women sat consoling one another and walked over to them.

Kim recognized one of the women as Job's twin sister Leslie. "Hi Leslie, my name is Kim, you may not remember me, but I'm an old friend of Job's from high school." Leslie looked up, immediately recognizing her. They had not seen each other in years, but Kim still looked the same. Leslie threw her arms around Kim. "Kim, what's going on?" Leslie questioned as she continued to weep. Kim didn't have an answer.

She let the tears that she'd been holding back fall. "Leslie, we need to tell Job what happened," Kim said as her voice cracked. "Will you come with me?" Kim asked. Leslie reached out for Anita's hand. "Kim, this is Anita, "Leslie said. "She lives with Job and his," she stopped short of finishing her sentence, realizing there is no longer a family. "Anita was the one who told us what happened," Leslie sniffed.

"The police came to the house hours ago, and Anita kept trying to reach Job at the office and on his cell phone, but when he didn't answer, she decided to just come to the office." "Hello Anita, I am so sorry to meet you under these circumstances," Kim said. Anita embraces Kim and Leslie.

"It's going to take all of our support to help Job get through this. We need to be strong for him," Anita says.

Kim nodded her head in agreement. When they reentered the conference room, Agent Williams dismissed everyone except Job and his lawyers. Job sat at the table with his head in his hands.

He was so concerned about his family. His assets were frozen, and his family was on the other side of the world alone with no money. Job had never in his life felt so helpless. He planned to call Mateo as soon as they wrapped up, so he doesn't have to worry Roni.

"Agent Williams, please forgive me, but this has been a very long day. I need to contact my family. Their plane landed over an hour ago. I'm sure my wife has called several times by now. I need to talk to my wife," Job pleaded.

Kim sat in the chair next to Job as he turned to face her. She sighed deeply before she looked into his eyes, fighting back her tears. "Kim, what's wrong?" Job asked. "Job I am so, so sorry, but we just received word that the plane your family was on…crashed shortly after takeoff."

Suddenly there was a ringing in Job's ears. Things started moving in slow motion. Job could see Kim's lips moving, but he did not hear the words she was saying. He looked around at the solemn expressions on the faces of everyone in the room before his eyes lock on Anita and Leslie.

He knew by the looks on their faces that this was indeed really happening. "I don't understand," Job said. "No, it can't be them," he said. "I watched the plane take off." Job stood and started pacing the floor. "No, it's the wrong plane I know it is, it has to be," he cried. "I wish that were the case." I really do Job," Kim said as tears began to fall down her face. "No, noooooo. It can't be, GOD PLEASE!" Job screamed. "PLEASE, PLEASE, PLEASE!" he cried.

Job dropped to his knees and was inconsolable as Leslie and Anita knelt by his side. "I need to see my family. Are they okay?" Job asked looking pleadingly into Kim's eyes. "Job, I'm sorry, but," before Kim could finish Job screams to the top of his lungs. "Please tell me this isn't happening. Please God, please." Anita stood next to him silently praying. Her own heart was breaking, but right now she needed to support him.

After several moments, Job got himself under control. "All of them?" he asked. Kim looks at him sadly as the tears continue to fall down her face. She closed her eyes and nodded yes. "Can I see them?" he asked in a fearfully calm voice. "Let me see what I can do," Kim said as she exited the room.

# CHAPTER THREE

Kim spoke with a friend at the Baltimore Medical Examiner's Office. Job would have to come to positively identify the bodies eventually anyway, so the examiner made an exception for Kim. As Kim relayed the message to Job, she could see the pain in his eyes. She could tell that none of them are in any state to be behind the wheel of a car and offered to drive them.

As they exited the elevator and walked toward the lobby, it was a ghost town. Not a single person was there. Job felt as if his legs were made of cement. Kim felt so sorry for him. In the blink of an eye, everything that Job knew to be normal had changed entirely. Every time Kim closed her eyes she saw the image of his family in her head.

The drive to the medical examiner's office was painfully quiet. Job kept having flashbacks of the last time he'd seen his wife and children. When they arrived, there was a heaviness that draped the car like a wet blanket. No one wanted to exit the vehicle, including Kim. She was hoping beyond hope that there had been a horrible mistake, but she knew that the bureau didn't make these kinds of mistakes.

Job finally opened the car door as the others followed. Before they head inside Anita asked them to hold hands and began to pray. As much as Job's heart ached, he continued to hold on to his belief that all of this was a part of God's ultimate plan no matter how much it was killing him on the inside.

After praying and shedding more tears, they entered the building one by one with Kim leading the group. As they arrived at the cold examination room, they noticed a man that they assume was the medical examiner and his assistant. They could tell by her red, puffy eyes that she'd been crying. Job looked at each sheet-covered gurney and immediately knew without even seeing them, that this was his family.

"Hi Eugene," Kim said. This is Jobias Arrington and his family." This was not the way that Eugene typically liked to conduct the identification process, but he thought having this man view the remains of his entire family via a monitor would be cold and impersonal.

Eugene hated this part of his job, but he knew that there would never be an easy way to handle this and he didn't want to postpone it any longer. "Right this way," Eugene said as he leads them to the gurneys. "Mr. Arrington before we begin let me inform you of the process. I'll remove the sheet from each gurney, and I need you to let me know if this is your decedent relative." Eugene placed his hand on Job's shoulder and looked up at him, ensuring that he understood. Job nodded.

"Please let me know if this is your wife, Veronica Denise Arrington." Job closed his eyes at the sight of the belly budge and bit his bottom lip to silence the scream he felt building up inside. Job would've fallen when Eugene pulled back the sheet had he and Kim not been standing there.

Job slowly nodded his head, gently touching her belly as tears flowed down his face. They moved to the next gurney, "Daniel Michael Arrington," Eugene said, and Job nodded again and rubbed his son's head. They moved to the next gurney, "Angel Precious Arrington," Eugene said. Job leaned over and began to weep.

He couldn't believe his baby-girl was gone. Job stands, wiped his eyes and took a deep breath as they lead him to the next gurney. Eugene cleared his throat, Kim looked at him and noticed tears in his eyes. "Aaron Avery

Arrington," Eugene said, Job smiled at his son and nodded, remembering their conversation from earlier that day.

They walked to the next gurney, "James Matthew Arrington," Eugene said as Job nods. Job closed his eyes, remembering the look on James' face. James wanted so much to make his father proud. Whenever he disappointed his father, it always seemed to affect him profoundly.

They walked over to the last two gurneys. "I'm so sorry sir, but we could not tell the twins apart." Job smiled, as he spoke for the first time since entering the room. "Most people can't tell the difference," he smiled. Eugene pulled both sheets back and stepped aside. Job stood between the two with the most sorrowful look that Kim had ever seen.

"This is Joshua Jeffrey Arrington," he said touching Joshua's head as he swallowed the lump in his throat, "and this is Jacob Amir Arrington," he said touching Jacob's head. "If you look closely, Jacob has a small dimple in his chin. Eugene grabbed a pen and wrote the boys' names on each tag.

"Thank you, sir," Eugene said. Eugene walked back to his desk as Kim, Leslie and Anita comforted Job. By this time, they were all crying. Kim hurt so much for them. Her mind drifted back to the photos in his office, showing a family so full of life and now they lay on these cold gurneys, void of the vibrant life shown in those photos.

Job couldn't take it any longer and dropped to the floor and screamed. The security officers ran to the door upon hearing his screams, but Eugene waved them away. After a short while Job composed himself and signed the documents needed for Eugene to issue their death certificates.

"Mr. Arrington, I cannot begin to tell you how sorry I am for your loss," Eugene said. Job nodded as he continued to look at the bodies of his family. "I have never been a God-fearing man. I mean I believe in a higher power, but that's as far as it went for me, until today.

I can't begin to imagine the pain that you must feel right now, but in my line of work, I deal with what you can see and prove, the facts if you will. I don't know how but I want you to know that your family did not suffer at all. The investigators detected unusually high levels of carbon monoxide.

"This is extremely unusual, but somehow the fumes on the plane allowed them to sleep right through the crash. They never even knew what happened Mr. Arrington.

What's even more shocking for me is that none of them have any broken bones or bruises.

"Not one person on the airliner had even a scratch or blemish yet the plane was completely destroyed. I have never seen anything like this in my entire life."

Job smiled, he knew that it was God. "Eugene, thank you so much. I needed to hear that," Job said hugging the older man. Eugene nodded his head as he stood aside to let them exit the room. "Thank you, Eugene," Kim said hugging him. "Anything for you Kim," he smiled.

Kim hugged Leslie briefly before she led them down the hall to exit the building. A few of the officers who worked the scene of the accident were also there. They offered Job words of comfort and condolences as they exited the building.

As they stepped out into the cool night air, Job took a deep breath and stood there for a moment. The thought of leaving his family in this cold, dark place was more than he could bear. Anita walked over to him, almost as if reading his mind, "To be absent from the body is to be present with the Lord," she said as she hugged him. Job took another deep breath and nodded as they all slowly walked back to the car. Job stared at the building for a few more moments before looking over to Kim.

"Well it's been a long day," Job said. "I guess we should head home." At the thought of home, Job felt his chest compress. That place would never again be a home to him. Job laid his head back on the headrest as the tears flowed down his face.

Kim started the ignition and slowly pulled away from the building. Job put his hand on the cold window as if somehow it would keep him connected to his family inside. Kim started driving back toward DC. She had no idea where Job lived, but she didn't want to bother him with directions now. After riding for a while, Job started giving Kim directions to the house. "Thank you so much for everything Kim, I appreciate you being here," Job said.

"It's not a problem at all Job. I wish I could be more helpful," Kim replied. "I will do my best to get them to relinquish your assets as soon as possible, but if you need anything at all in the meantime, please don't hesitate to call me." "Thank you," Job said, "but we will be fine."

As they arrived at the gatehouse, they were all quiet as Job's security team recognized him and allowed them through. Anita was the first to exit the car. Job and Leslie were next, followed by Kim. "Wow you have an amazing home," Kim said. Job smiled, "Thanks. Roni picked it out. She loved this house."

For the first time since hearing of the accident, Job was able to speak his wife's name. "Would you like to come in?" Job asked. "Umm well it's late, and you guys need to get some rest," Kim said. "You're welcome to stay the night," Job said. "We have plenty of extra rooms, and I'm not comfortable with you driving home at such a late hour." "Thank you, but I will be fine," Kim said.

"Kim get yourself in this house," Anita said from the doorway. "It's 3 AM, and you are not driving anywhere at this time of morning so come on." Kim laughed, "Alrighty then." "Yeah, it's no use fighting it. Anita always gets her way," Job said, shaking his head.

"That's right," Anita said, "now come on to the kitchen so I can fix us something to eat." "I'm not hungry," Job and Leslie say at the same time. "I didn't ask if you're hungry," Anita said, "You need to eat. Now sit." "Yes ma'am, they both utter," Kim smiled as Anita winked at her. After they finish eating, Job and Leslie head to their bedrooms while Anita showed Kim to one of the guest rooms. "Thank you so much for letting me stay the night. I didn't trust myself driving either. I was going to grab a couple of hours of sleep in my car."

"We've had enough tragedy for one day, and there's plenty of room in this house," Anita said. "Thank you so much," Kim said as she reached out to hug Anita. For some reason, Anita reminded Kim so much of her mom. "Aww, baby it's no trouble at all. There are clean towels, washcloths and toiletries in the bathroom and some drinks in the mini fridge. If you need anything else, I am right across the hall. Now you get some sleep."

"Goodnight Anita," Kim said. "Goodnight Kim," Anita said as she turned to exit the room. Anita nearly bumped into Leslie as she exited the room. "I'm so sorry Anita," Leslie apologized. "I just wanted to give Kim some clean clothes for tomorrow." "Thank you so much, Leslie. I appreciate all of your hospitality," Kim said accepting the clothing. "You're welcome," Leslie responded solemnly before hugging Kim and heading back to her bedroom.

Kim softly closed the door, trying to wrap her head around the magnitude of losing your entire family in one devastating moment. Her mom's death nearly destroyed her. Kim showered as her strong facade finally crumbled.

Sobs escape from her small frame until she had no tears left.

Sleep eluded everyone including Job who lay in bed alone for the first time in 21 years. He could still smell the scent of his wife's perfume. He hugged her pillow tightly, crying as his heart ached for his family. Leslie was in her room curled up in a chair as she stared at the last photo she had taken with her niece and nephews at Christmas. Anita was on her knees praying for Job and the family and asking Roni to watch over him.

Kim tossed and turned throughout the night. She kept seeing the family photo on Job's desk every time she closed her eyes. Kim was haunted by the images of a happy family that she had never known yet felt so profoundly connected to for some reason. She never in a million years thought that this was how her day would end. Her heart ached as she thought of the look on Job's face. She had never seen him look so broken. Kim prayed that God would comfort and strengthen him.

# CHAPTER FOUR

As the birds started chirping, Kim got up to shower and dress. It was evident that she would not be getting any sleep today. Kim quietly exited the room, led to the kitchen by the heavenly aroma of bacon and coffee. As she rounded the corner, Anita was busy putting biscuits in the oven. Kim looked at the table filled with bacon, sausage, home fries and waffles and her mouth started watering. She didn't realize how hungry she had been. "Good morning," Anita smiled as she handed Kim a cup of coffee. "Thanks Anita," Kim said. Are you always up this early?" Kim asked, sipping the hot coffee. "You know what they say, the early bird gets the worm," Anita smiled.

Kim smiled back at her thinking once again of her mom. "Job goes running every morning for an hour at 5:30 AM so he should be back shortly," Anita said. "Do you think he'll" ...before Kim could finish, Job walked in the door sweaty from his run. Anita smiled at Kim who just shook her head. "Good morning," Job said as he entered the kitchen and saw Kim sitting at the table drinking coffee.

For a brief second, he thought about the morning before. Exactly 24 hours ago his wife and children were alive and well. He visibly flinched at the pain as the memories came flooding back to him. Anita knew exactly what he was thinking. She turned her back as she too fought back tears. "Excuse me for a moment," she said as she left the room. "Did you sleep well?" Job asked, clearing his throat and trying to block out the image from yesterday of his wife and son. "Not really," Kim smiled sadly. "Yeah, neither did I," Job sighed.

Job and Kim were sitting at the table attempting to eat breakfast; both lost in their thoughts. "I know the next few days are going to be pretty hectic, so I spoke with Agent Williams earlier, and you won't have to worry about anyone bothering you for the next week," Kim said. "Thank you so much," Job answered.

"Well I'm going get out of your hair, I know things are going to be crazy but seriously if you need anything, to talk or to not talk, just let me know," Kim said. "Thank you, Kimmy, I will. Are you sure you're okay to drive home?" he asked. "Yes, I'm fine," she smiled at his use of her childhood nickname.

"I normally function pretty well off 3-4 hours of sleep a day, so I'll just run home and grab a catnap." "That's not very healthy," Job said. "I know, but I don't get much sleep these days," she said. "Okay, well let me walk you out," Job said as he stood.

As they walked to the truck, Job hugged Kim and opened the door for her. As she got in, she noticed a cell phone lying on the passenger seat. "Is this your phone?" Kim asked. "Oh yes thank you," Job said. "I would've wondered where I left this. Please drive safely and give me a call when you get in." "I will," Kim said.

Kim noticed that there are several news reporters camped out across the street from the gatehouse as she drove off. As much as she hated it, legally there was nothing she can do to stop them since they were not actually on Job's property.

"Good morning Mrs. Godwin," the young attendant at the gate said as Kim stopped at his request. Kim was somewhat puzzled that he knew her name. "Good morning ma'am, my name is Sean." Job gave us your name during his run and instructed me to sign you in, so you don't have to worry about checking in when you return," "Thank you so much," Kim said, accepting the pass.

As Kim drove away, she smiled as she thought about how far they'd come from their old neighborhood. She was proud of Job and had followed his career throughout the years. When Kim heard about the investigation into his organization, she put in a request to work with the agents handling the case. She knew Job would never be guilty of something like this. He'd always been an upstanding man, and no dollar amount would ever change that.

As Job returned to the house, he saw Anita turn to avoid making eye contact with him. He walked over to her and turned her to face him. He hugged her and held her close. "I don't know what's wrong with me," Anita said as she held him tightly while the tears continued to fall. "I should be rejoicing; they have gone on to glory. I'm just going to miss my precious babies."

Job held his head back to keep his tears from falling. "Me too Anita, me too." I know dad is helping Roni take care of them for me though," he choked, referring to his father who passed away two years earlier. "Ha!" Anita laughed, "More like getting on their nerves with those jokes." Job began to laugh. It had been a while since he'd thought about his dad's jokes.

His father told the corniest jokes he'd ever heard. He thought his second calling was to be a comedian. "Anita, I needed that laugh. Thank you. We are going to get through this," Job sighed. "When dad passed, I thought I'd never get over that pain, but it gets easier every day."

"I still miss him, but I know he's in a better place." "Yes Lord, this world is not our home," Anita said. "We forget that sometimes getting so caught up in this world," Job agreed. "I'm going to take a shower. I'll be down shortly." "Okay baby take your time," Anita said. "It's going to be a long day." "Don't I know it," Job said, shaking his head.

# CHAPTER FIVE

Job walked up the stairs slowly as visions of the previous day flooded his memory. Job's heart was heavy as he walked by all the bedrooms he had just visited the day before. He sat on Jacob's bed, looking around the room at various trains and Legos that he'd helped his sons build.

As the tears fell down his face, he began to thank God for giving him the short but precious time with his boys. He softly closed the door as he exited their room and walked to Angel's bedroom. He caught himself just before he knocked on the door as he usually would and slowly opened her door.

The smell of her perfume still lingered in the room. Job noticed the picture from their last date night on her nightstand. She was the spitting image of her mom. He remembered thinking about how she was growing up so fast. He took the picture with him as he left the room.

He entered Aaron and James' room and smiled when he saw James' boxing gloves on his bed. "I'm sure he tried to pack them for the trip," Job thought. He turned and saw the keys to the convertible on Aaron's nightstand. He picked up the keys and puts them in his pocket before heading to Daniel's room.

As he entered his room, the first thing he saw was a picture of the two of them on the wall. Daniel caught a 70-pound catfish during the summer, and a local newspaper photographed them. Daniel was so proud that day.

Job closed his eyes and smiled as the memories came back to him. He was going to miss his family so much. As Job exited the room, he looked back at the smile on his son's face. He was so grateful that he has such beautiful memories with his family. As he entered his bedroom, he headed to the bathroom to shower.

As Job exits the shower, he knelt and began to pray. "Lord, I don't understand this, and I'm not even going to pretend that I do but I trust you, Lord. Please take care of my family until I get there and please give me the strength to bear this great loss."

As Job finished dressing, there was a soft knock at his door. "Come in," he answered. Leslie entered the room and walked over and hugged him. "Did you get any sleep at all?" Job asked. Leslie shook her head no.

She looked around the room at the pictures of the family all around the room and laid her head on Job's shoulder. Job pulled her close. "Sis, it's going to be okay," Job said as he hugged her tightly. "We are going to get through this together, I promise." "It's just too much Job," Leslie cried. "I don't understand why this is happening," Leslie said sitting down on the bed. "I don't know why either sis, but we can't focus on that. What is that scripture dad used to quote?"

"The Lord gives, and the Lord also takes away." Leslie nodded as she sniffled. "All we can do is try to focus on the good times we had with them," Job said. "You know how the enemy works. He attempts to break us down, but we must stand strong. Getting through this won't be easy. I honestly can't tell you how I am going to get through the next five minutes let alone the rest of my life, but God knows. He equipped us for this very moment before we were born. I have to have faith and trust that this is happening for a reason way beyond my understanding," Job said as tears fell down his face. "We had them for a while, and I guess it is their time to go home."

"All I can focus on is continuing to live right so I can join them when that time comes. Leslie grabbed a tissue from the dresser and wiped her eyes and nose. "You're right," she said with a big sigh. "The family is downstairs waiting for you." Job closed his eyes and sighed. "Who's down there?" "Everyone," Leslie said. "Mom, Marcus, Jonathan, Carlos, David, Danielle, Jerry, and Adrienne. Oh, and Eli called earlier too, he's picking up Billy, and Alphonso and they'll be here little later this afternoon." Job sighed deeply once again. "Okay, I guess I should've expected this."

Well, I need to get started on the arrangements. "Do you remember the name of the company that handled Dad's arrangements?" Job asked. "I liked them a lot." "Yes, it's Kingdom Haven Funeral Home. I can call Michael if you want," Leslie said. "Yeah, that's it," Job said. "I want them to handle everything. Umm…who's Michael?" Job asked.

Leslie could not contain her smile as she began to blush. "He's the director of the funeral home. We stayed in touch after dad's service. "Is that right?" Job asked. "Is it serious?" "Well, right now we're taking things slow, but I think it's getting there," she smiled. "Why didn't you say anything?" Job asked with a grin on his face. Job watched the smile fade from his sister's face. "I told Roni about him," Leslie said quietly.

Job hugged his twin tightly. He knew how much she loved Roni and the kids. "Come on sis let's get down there before they start coming up here." As Job and Leslie headed down to greet the rest of the family, they could hear them talking. His family had always been lively. "Hey, I waited here for hours for you yesterday, and I've been calling you all night," his brother Marcus said, noticing his brother and sister enter the kitchen.

"Things were a bit crazy as you can imagine," Job said. "We didn't get home until early this morning," Job said, grabbing a bottle of water from the fridge. I guess all the calls and texts drained my battery. We can discuss the particulars later, but I would like you to handle the service." Marcus teared up at the thought of eulogizing his sister-in-law, niece, and nephews. "No problem Job. You know I've got you." Marcus followed in their father's footsteps and had taken over as senior pastor at their church. Everyone hugged and kissed Job as he made his way around to greet everyone.

# CHAPTER SIX

The next five days were a whirlwind. People were in and out of the house all day long. There were so many food and floral deliveries that Job lost count. The phone seemed to ring nonstop with calls from family, friends and business associates and the news reporters are still camped out across the street from his home. His company woes and the death of his family were major news.

The night before the funeral, Job dreamt that Roni and the children were in the most beautiful place he has ever seen, and they were happy. He woke as Roni kisses his lips. When Job opened his eyes, he realized that he'd been crying in his sleep. He could still feel her lips on his. "Thank you, Lord. I needed that," Job prayed.

Job got out of bed and prayed as he did every morning. "Lord, thank you for your strength. Please help me as I lean not on my own understanding, but on your grace and mercy. For my strength is made perfect in weakness. Job decided not to go on his run today. He looked at himself in the mirror, thanking God in advance for the endurance to persevere through this day.

Job entered the kitchen where his family had already gathered waiting for him. They hugged and prepared for breakfast as Marcus blessed the food. He ended the prayer by saying, "*God, I know that you have a plan and we will see your goodness prevail, be it in this life or the next one. Jesus says blessed are they that mourn for they will be comforted, and we ask for your comfort Lord, this day and the many days to come, Amen.*" Job wanted so much for his mother to understand that. Angela exited the room as soon as they began praying. When Job's father died, his mom withdrew from the Lord.

She felt that they'd done everything in God's Will and she was still angry at God for taking her husband. Job didn't understand why this was happening. He was a dedicated servant and tried his best to live righteously, but he still would never turn his back on God. He knew that God had a purpose and plan for his life.

It felt surreal as the family prepared to depart for the home-going service. Job felt like he was hovering over his body watching all of this happen to someone else as he entered the limo adorned with the funeral home's logo. The ride to the church felt so fast. Job wanted to drag it out as long as he possibly could to keep them with him.

Although, he knew that they would always be with him. He had once heard a woman speak about this portal in Heaven that allowed families to look down to earth to encourage their families to stand firm. Job knew without a doubt that his family would be rooting him on. Telling him to stand strong and trust in the Lord. Job believed that his dream was a confirmation from the Lord that they were okay.

As they arrived at the church, hundreds of people were already gathered. Job had anticipated a large crowd, but this was beyond anything he had expected. He knew how much he and his family were all loved, but this was a bit overwhelming. As he exited the limo, somehow, he linked eyes with Kim. He motioned for her to wait for him. As he got closer, he hugged her and thanked her for coming. "I want you to sit with my family," Job stated. Kim nodded her head holding back her tears.

As they entered the church, Kim attempted to maneuver her way toward the back just as Carlos reached out and pulled her close to him. Carlos was too young to remember Kim when she and Job dated, but he met her the day after the accident and realized exactly why his brother fell in love with her. She was one of the sweetest people that he'd ever met. Carlos held Kim's hand tightly as they lined up to enter the church.

The parishioners all stood as the family walked toward the front of the church to view the bodies. The six beautiful, pearl white caskets were spread out like a fan near the altar. Kim and Carlos held on to each other. The image of such a tragedy would be forever engraved in Kim's mind. One of the ministers began to speak as they continued their tread down the aisle.

*"Lamentations 3:22, Through the Lord's mercies we are not consumed, because His compassions fail not. They are new every morning. The Lord gave us great gifts, and the Lord chose to take them away. Blessed be the name of the Lord for He is good and worthy to be praised. We praise through the pain because we know that to be absent from the body is to be with the Lord."*

Job and his family took their time to view each casket lovingly. Several times Job felt as if he was about to break down, but he composed himself, closed his eyes and thought about his dream. After he took his seat, Job held his head down as he softly wept as his mother and sister comforted him.

During the remainder of the homegoing service there was laughter and tears as people share memories about Roni and the kids. Job made his way to the podium with all his brothers standing alongside him. Job sighed deeply. "Roni would've loved this," he said, looking around at the huge crowd. "It makes me feel so good to see how much my family was loved and it brings me great comfort to know that Roni was a fantastic mother to my children in this life and will continue to take care of them in next one.

Last night I dreamt of them" he said as his voice cracked and tears fell down his face. "They were in the most beautiful place I had ever seen and they were happy. For me, that was confirmation that they are with the Lord. I am going to miss them more than words can say. There is not a second that they will not be in my heart, but I humbly give them back to the Lord. I thank each one of you for your thoughts and prayers during this difficult time, and I pray that the Lord bless and keep you all."

Job hugged his brothers and walked off the pulpit just before the closing of the caskets. Job stood next to the coffins as *I Shall Wear a Crown* began to echo through the church as his brothers walked down the aisle holding pillows with crowns on top. Job took a deep breath as the tears started to fall from his eyes.

As his brothers made their way to the altar. Job removed a crown from each pillow and placed a crown upon the heads of his wife and each of his children, including the twins who shared a casket. After crowning his wife and children, Job kissed the top of his children's heads and his wife's lips one final time before helping his brother's close their caskets.

As Job closed his wife's casket last, he laid his head on her coffin and began to weep as his brothers, and the elders of the church surrounded him and began praying for him. There was not a dry eye in the church. It broke Kim's heart to watch the pain that Job and his family had to endure.

# CHAPTER SEVEN

After the funeral, Job felt a bit overwhelmed. The family and a few friends came back to the house after the repast. Job decided to go for a ride alone. He hadn't had time to be alone since the accident.

As he exited the driveway Marvin Sapp's *"My Testimony"* began to play. Job smiled as he drove the short distance to a local park near the water where he and Roni often took the children. As he exited the car, he was surprised to see Kim sitting on a nearby bench.

Kim jumped when Job called out to her. She was so caught up in her thoughts that she had not seen him arrive. "I'm sorry I didn't mean to scare you," Job apologized. "I'm fine," Kim replied. "I didn't hear you walk up and you just startled me a little. What are you doing here?" she asked.

"I had to get out of the house," Job said, rubbing his head. "I know my family and friends love me, but I needed some time alone. It's beginning to be a bit too much. I didn't know you knew about this park," he said changing the subject.

"Yeah, I actually found it by mistake the day I left your house," Kim laughed. "I got a little turned around and ended up here," she said as she looked around at the beautiful sight. "I love this place. It's so serene here." "I agree," Job said, but you really shouldn't be out here alone."

There has been a couple of attacks in the past." Kim smiled. "Thank you, but the FBI trained me very well to take care of myself, sir." "Oh yeah, I forgot you're Ms. Big Bad FBI Lady now," Job laughed. Kim laughed as she lightly punched him in the arm. "I see you still have that smart mouth," Kim laughed. There was a silence that hung in the air before they both tried to speak at once.

They both laughed nervously. "You first," Job smiled. "We haven't had time to talk with everything going on," Kim smiled. "I just wanted to know how you're holding up." Job sighed deeply, "Well, I have my good and bad days."

"I know God has a plan and I have to trust it. I don't like it or understand it, but I trust Him. I just…I miss them so much." Kim was at his side immediately as tears fell down his face. "Job I truly cannot imagine the pain you must feel. If there is anything that I can do, please let me know." "Thank you," he said, staring at the lake. "And thank you so much for coming today and helping out with the repast," Job said changing the subject again. "Absolutely," Kim responded, "I would not have been anywhere else. That's what family is for."

Job nodded. "Well, I need to get going. I have a medical appointment at 4:30." "Today? You can't reschedule?" Kim asked. "I could've, but I just wanted to get it over with," Job said. "Is everything okay?" Kim asked. "Well," Job sighed, "I need to keep this between us, but I've had these headaches for the past month. My doctor decided to do a CT scan and noticed an abnormality. He had me come in for some additional tests last week, and the results came back yesterday. I hate to ask and please feel free to say no, but would you mind coming with me?"

"Of course, I'll come with you," Kim answered. "Ok, you can follow me over since the park will be closing shortly," Job said. "Ok and thank you." "I appreciate this," Job said. "Jobi if you don't stop thanking me," Kim said, using her special nickname for him growing up, we're family. You'd do the same thing for me." Job nodded his head in agreement. "I will be sure to drive nice and slow, so I don't lose you, Mrs. Daisy," he joked. "Whatever," Kim said laughing. "You're the one who taught me how to drive so what does that say about you?" she laughed. "Whatever," Job laughed.

# CHAPTER EIGHT

A short time later they arrived at the medical building. Kim walked over to Job as they exited their cars. "Wow, this building is beautiful," Kim said. My doctors' offices never look like this." "I forgot to tell you, Mack from high school is my doctor," Job said smiling. "He and his brother run this practice. A lot of local athletes come here which is why it's so fancy."

"Hold up," Kim said. "Waterhead Mack? Are you serious?" Kim laughed. "Yep in the flesh, he had a whole lotta knowledge up in that cranium, who knew?" Job said as they both laughed, entering the building. Job said a silent prayer on the elevator, but for some reason, he wasn't afraid. He knew that whatever the outcome, it was God's Will for his life.

As they entered the suite, the front desk receptionist greeted Job by name. She looked so familiar to Kim. The woman came from behind the desk and hugged Job. "The service was beautiful Job. How are you holding up?" she asked. "I am doing the best that I can Keisha," Job sighed. Keisha turned and looked at Kim, and that's when it hit Kim.

She and Keisha shared the same homeroom class all four years in high school. "Oh my gosh Keisha I didn't even recognize you. You look amazing!" Kim exclaimed. "Thank you girl, I lost 50 pounds after Mack and I got married. I couldn't take it anymore. It's good to see you again. I didn't even know you were back in town," Keisha said. "Yeah, I've been back for about two years now," Kim smiled. It felt so good to see her friends from high school.

She moved around quite a bit during her tenure with the FBI, but Maryland would always be home to her. Job looked at her curiously. "Why didn't you call me?" he asked. "That would've been a little awkward don't you think," Kim smirked. Job thought about it, "Yeah I guess you're right, but still it would've been nice to know you were in town.

"Look at me, I'm so busy catching up that I'm not even doing my job," Keisha said, noticing two more patients had come into the office. "Job you can go on back, Mack is expecting you," Keisha said. "Keisha is there a restroom around here I can use?" Kim asked. "Yes, it's out the door and to the right, you can't miss it," Keisha instructed, walking over to greet the incoming patients.

As Kim washed her hands, she stares at her reflection in the mirror. "Lord please continue to strengthen Job. Ease this burden on his shoulders and guide him during this painful time." As she reentered the office, Keisha looked over at her and smiled as she spoke with another patient.

Kim sat down and selected a magazine from the small table. Shortly after, Keisha called Kim to the receptionist's desk. "Mack wants to see you," Keisha said. "Just go through those doors, take a left and the first right." "Okay, thanks." As Kim walked through the office, she couldn't help but marvel at the beautiful office.

Kim walked toward the door with the gold nameplate engraved, Dr. William Mackey and knocked. "Come in," Mack answered. Mack came from around his desk and hugged Kim when she entered his office. "It's good to see you, Kim. I wanted to say hello earlier," he stopped himself as he glanced over at Job.

"Well, it's really good seeing you," Mack said. Kim noticed the look on Job's face. "What's wrong?" she asked, looking back and forth from Job to Mack. "Have a seat Kim," Job said. "Job you are seriously scaring me," Kim said. "What's going on? People never tell you to sit down when they have good news."

Kim sat down beside Job and tried to calm herself down. "Job please just tell me." Kim pleaded. "Well," Job began as he took her hand, "that spot Mack found is a pretty big tumor." Kim swallowed hard as her heart felt as if it is going to beat out of her chest.

"Okay, what do we need to do?" she asked. "Sadly, there is nothing we can do" Job answered. Kim could not believe her ears. Job was one of her dearest friends. This diagnosis could not be the end for him. It just couldn't be.

At this point, Mack jumped in, "Kimmy trust me I've looked at this from several different angles and called in colleagues from all over the world. Right now, the best I can do is make sure that he's comfortable," Mack choked. "I truly wish I could tell you something different. I've done everything that I know to do and then some." Mack looked up toward the ceiling in an attempt to stop the tears that had gathered in his eyes from falling. Job had always been one of his closest friends.

Mack wouldn't even have his practice if Job hadn't loaned him the money. Mack loved Job like a big brother. He felt like such a failure because he couldn't find a way to help him. "Kimmy, it's okay," Job said as he rubbed her shoulder. "I trust God completely. If this is how it's supposed to go down, then it is what it is, but I am not giving up."

Kim could no longer hold back her emotions and began to cry. She had loved this man all her life. Kim could not bear the thought of losing Job. "I...I don't even know what to say," Kim stuttered. "There's nothing to say, Kimmy. I've had a great, amazing life", Job smiled.

"I had an amazing, beautiful wife who loved me and an opportunity to love her back and six amazing children that I love more than life itself." "I have been able to live out my dream career. I've been blessed beyond measure. I can't have sunshine all the time and if this is God's Will for my life so be it. He didn't owe me anything but gave me everything. Everything will work out. I promise," Job said.

Kim nodded, not knowing how else to respond. Mack cleared his throat, "Job I sent a couple of prescriptions down to the pharmacy. They should help with the pain. If not, please let me know, and I'll prescribe something else. We have counselors here for you and your family." Job smiled. "Thanks Mack, but I think I will take this one to the Wonderful Counselor." Mack nodded his head and walked around to hug Job.

"Well you know we are here if you need anything at all," Mack said. "Thanks for everything," Job responded and stop looking like somebody kicked your cat, Mack. One of two things will happen. God will heal me completely or he's decided it's time for me to be with my family. Either way, I'm okay with His decision, okay?" Mack sighed. "You take care of yourself Waterhead," Job laughed trying to lighten the mood.

"I'm hungry all of a sudden," Job said. "Want to grab a bite?" he asked Kim. "Umm sure," Kim answered. "Okay Mack I'll give you a call next week," Job said. "Okay and don't forget to pick up your prescriptions" Mack reminded him. "I'm so glad you said something Mack, I had already forgotten," Job laughed as he exited the office.

# CHAPTER NINE

Job and Kim waved goodbye to Keisha before heading to the pharmacy to pick up his prescriptions. They decided to go to TGI Friday's after picking up his medicine. Job and Kim arrived at the restaurant, which was unusually crowded for a Wednesday night.

While waiting for their table, Job noticed one of his employees and waved him over. "Hey Job, how are you?" Lee asked. "I'm blessed, Lee." "I'm sorry that I couldn't make the funeral," Lee apologized. "It's not a problem Lee, I'm sure I didn't see half the people that were there. I know you were there in spirit though."

"I'm sorry Kim, please forgive me for being so rude. Lee this is Kim, one of my dearest friends in the whole world. Lee is one of the best IT guys in the business. If you ever have a computer issue, this is your man." Lee smiled at the compliment. "It's a pleasure to meet you, Ms. Kim." "It's a pleasure meeting you as well, Lee," Kim smiled. Job could see the concern on Lee's face.

"I haven't heard anything about when we'll be able to get back to work, but please be assured that I will be on the phone first thing tomorrow morning and see if I can get some answers," Job said. "Thanks Job. I appreciate that. Please know that everyone is praying for you," Lee said.

"That I do know, and I thank you all for your prayers and support during everything that's been going on." "Arrington, party of two," the hostess called. "Well that's us," Job said. "Okay," Lee said, "You two enjoy your meal and have a good night." "You too Lee, nice to meet you," Kim responded. As they were seated and looking at their menus, Kim remarked, "Your employees love you." "I love them too," Job beamed. "When I first thought about branching out on my own, I knew that I wanted to create an extended family, not a building full of employees.

Too bad I didn't do a better job when I picked Samuel." "Hey, you can't blame yourself for that," Kim said. "He didn't act alone which made the deception a lot easier to cover up." Job shook his head. "I guess I should not be too surprised since Samuel hand-picked the entire department himself."

"I still can't believe I was so late catching on though and how could he come into work every day and look these people in their face knowing that he was stealing from them? I just don't get it. It makes me feel stupid."

"Job stop that," Kim demanded. "You are far from stupid okay? You just trusted the wrong people. We've all been there," she said as she blinked back the tears that had formed in her eyes.

"Hey, are you okay?" Job asked as he touched her hand. "We've been so focused on my life that we haven't had a chance to catch up." Kim took a sip of water before speaking. "I promise we will talk about everything soon enough. Just not tonight okay?" Kim pleaded.

"Okay," Job conceded, not wanting to press the issue, as he picked up the menu. "I know what I'm having," he said. "Let me guess, the Jack Daniel's Ribs and

Shrimp," Kim laughed. Job started laughing with her. "You know it," he sang.

"You know I'm glad that you came with me," Job said. Kim smiled. "Me too. I would've been sick at the thought of you dealing with this all alone." "I know, but I didn't want to burden my family until I knew what it was for certain. They have been through enough the last couple of years to last a lifetime."

"The hardest part is going to be telling them. God knows I love them, but sometimes having a big family can be a bit much." "I'm sure it can," Kim agreed. "I always wished I had a brother and sister though. It's no picnic being an only child." "I have eight…pick one," Job laughed. "You are so crazy," Kim laughed, shaking her head.

"Seriously though," Job said, "I'd like you to be there when I tell them if you don't mind. I need as much support as possible." "Are you sure?" Kim questioned. "Absolutely," Job replied. "You're family."

"I think I'm just going to invite the entire family and a few close friends over and tell everyone at once. I think it'll be easier dealing with one huge reaction than having to tell everyone individually." "I'd have to agree with you there," Kim said. They continued to chat as their beverages and food arrived.

"Thank you so much for dinner," Kim said as Job walked her to her car. "I'll be praying for you," she said hugging him. "You better be," Job laughed. "Job seriously, it's never a problem," Kim said. "Anything you need at all, I'm just a phone call away. Please don't forget to take your meds as soon as you get home. I saw you cringe a few times during dinner." "You noticed that huh?" Job asked, rubbing his temples. "I sure did. Please take care of yourself Job." "I will," he promised. "Drive safely."

"You too Job, goodnight," Kim said as she drove off. Kim did her best all through dinner to be strong for Job, but she broke the second that she exited the parking lot. Job was one of the most faithful and honorable men that she has ever known. It broke her heart to watch him suffer. She could only imagine the emotional turmoil that he must be going through, and now he had to deal with this horrible diagnosis. She prayed for him and his family during her drive home.

# CHAPTER TEN

As Job drove home, he decided to plan a BBQ for Saturday to tell everyone about his diagnosis. As he turned into the driveway, Anita and the rest of the family rushed out of the house. "Job are you trying to give me a heart attack?" she asked. "We were so worried about you," Leslie added as she hugged her brother. "Yeah, why didn't you answer your phone?" David questioned.

"Okay okay," Job said holding up his hands. "I can't answer all of your questions at once. I'm sorry that I worried you. I just needed to get away for a while. I went to the park to get away, and I ran into Kim. We talked for a while before going to dinner. I'm sorry. I didn't mean to worry you." They all hugged Job. "I'm glad you're all still here though," Job said. "I was thinking of having a BBQ on Saturday. What do you think?"

Job loved to grill in any weather. They'd had numerous family BBQs in the sunroom. They were all excited that Job wanted to host a BBQ. Marcus agreed to buy the ribs, and Leslie said she'd bring the sodas and ice.

Anita decided to make her infamous potato salad and mac & cheese.

"Okay well we can finalize the details tomorrow, I'm exhausted," Job said as he yawned. "Okay baby, get some rest," Anita said. Job kissed her on the cheek. "I will." "Job do you mind if I stay the night again?" Leslie asked. "Of course not, and since when do you ever ask?" Job teased as he hugged her.

"Let's have breakfast after my run tomorrow morning." "That sounds great," Leslie said. "You mind if I go running with you?" Leslie asked. Job stepped back and looked at Leslie cautiously. "Ummm who are you and what have you done with my twin sister?" Job teased.

Leslie laughed. "I'm serious. I need to get in shape anyway." "Okay, that would be nice. See you at 5:30" Job smiled, kissing her goodnight. That was usually Job's God time, but he didn't mind making an exception for his sister. "Ugh AM?" Leslie groaned. Job laughed as he hugged the rest of his family before heading off to his room.

As Job entered his bedroom, he noticed several copies of the obituary laying on his dresser. He kicked off his shoes and laid back across the bed as he read his families' obituary. He couldn't bear to look at it during the service. As he flipped the pages, he read the kind words many people had written about his family.

He was amazed at the time and work it must've taken to complete this so soon. He'd have to talk to Leslie to find out who did this. He wanted to thank them personally. There were pictures included that he had completely forgotten all about like the photos from their annual family ski trip to Beaver Creek, CO and a few pictures taken during their wedding.

After Job finished reading the obituary, he closed the booklet, holding it to his chest as the tears rolled down his face onto the bed as he slowly drifted off to sleep with visions of his family in his head.

Job was shocked to find his sister waiting for him in the kitchen the next morning. Leslie was leaning against the counter when Job entered the kitchen. "You okay sis?" he smirked, noticing that she could barely keep her eyes open. "Yes," she yawned. IHOP is keeping me motivated," she laughed. Job laughed. "IHOP huh? Okay, well come on and earn your IHOP."

Job and Leslie enjoyed their run. As they walked back to the house, they noticed several news cameras arrive and start setting up their cameras. "I cannot wait for them to latch onto a new piece of news," Leslie said. "I know," Job agreed. "At least we can keep them off the property. How have you been doing?" Job asked. Leslie fought back tears as she looked at him.

"Leslie, I know how close you were to Roni and the children," Job said. "I realize that this is just as big a loss for you as it is for me. I want to make sure you're okay." Leslie hugged her brother. "I love you so much Job. I'm dealing with it as well as I can. I try to focus on the good times, but I miss them so much." "You and me both sis, but life goes on whether we want it to or not." As they entered the house, they each headed off to shower and change for breakfast.

Job and Leslie had a great time at breakfast. Job missed his quality time with Leslie. He had always been closer to her than the other brothers and sisters since they were little. As they returned to the house, another floral delivery van was leaving.

Job laughed to himself thinking he could start his own floral business with all the flowers in the house. There were also tons of cards and letters from extended family members, colleagues past and present, college acquaintances and the like. Job was very well liked and respected and known for his character and integrity. Job wasn't ready to go through everything just yet. His cell phone began ringing just as he headed to his home office to do some work.

"Good morning Kim," Job said, seeing her name appear on the caller ID. "Hi Job, I'm so sorry, but can you come down to the office today? There are a few minor details that need to be resolved." "Sure," Job said, "How's 1:00?" "That's fine," Kim said. "Okay, I will see you shortly.

By the way, I'm inviting everyone over for a BBQ on Saturday. I would love for you to come over if you're free." "Sure, is there anything I can bring?" Kim asked. "Actually yes, do you still make that banana pudding you used to make in high school?" Kim laughed, thinking about how much Job loved her banana pudding.

"I have not made it in a very long time, but I'm sure I can whip up a couple of batches." Job's mouth began to water just thinking about it. "Great! Well, I will see you shortly." "Okay, thank you for the invite," Kim said. "Of course," Job smiled, "I'll see you in a few."

# CHAPTER ELEVEN

When Job reached the offices of the FBI building, he was more than a little anxious. He had done nothing wrong, but he also knew that families depended on him and he wanted to get this situation resolved as soon as possible for their sake. After two hours, Job was more than exhausted and ready to go home. The last week had been emotionally and mentally draining for him.

The investigators finally wrapped up and told Job they'd call him if they had additional questions. "I'm sorry Job," Kim apologized. We're trying to get this resolved ASAP. I know it's a lot on you. This is one time when I hate doing my job." "It's a lot I won't even lie about that," Job agreed. "But there are so many vultures out there and I'd rather them be extremely thorough with me than miss something with the next guy. I have faith that the truth will come out," Job said.

"How do you keep this positive attitude?" Kim asked. "My faith is strong, but like the man in the Bible, I have been asking the Lord to help my unbelief," Kim smiled. "I'm not going to pretend it doesn't get hard because it does," Job said. "I can't tell you how many nights I cry myself to sleep, but they say God doesn't give you more than you can bear and to be honest if you had told me last year that all of this would be happening I'd still be standing I would've thought you were crazy, but look at me. I'm still here, and I'm still standing," Job smiled. Kim nodded in agreement, "Yes you are. I wish I could've met them."

Job smiled bright, "They would've loved you. I told Roni about you. She always wanted to meet the woman that had my heart first." Kim swallowed the lump in her throat, "I'm sure I would've loved them too," she smiled.

"Well let me get going," Job said. "I've had to go home and pick up Anita. She doesn't trust me to get everything on her list. That woman I tell you," Job laughed. "I like her, she is a sweetheart," Kim said. "She is amazing," Job smiled, "I don't know what I would've done without her this past week and a half. God always puts the right people in our lives at the right times, present company included," he smiled. "I don't think that is by coincidence." "I've been thinking the same thing," Kim agreed.

"When I left town, I promised myself that I would never come back, but in the last few years something has been pulling me back." "That's how God works," Job said. "I know one thing. I have some questions for him when I do see him," Job laughed sarcastically. "That makes two of us," Kim smiled. "Well, I will let you go so you can head to the store. Are you sure you don't need me to bring anything else?" "Yes, we have everything else covered." "Great, I will see you on Saturday then," Kim said. "Okay, you be safe," Job said. "Thank you," Kim smiled, "I will. You do the same."

Job watched as Kim returned to the building. He knew they'd have to talk soon. Job had been so preoccupied lately, but he didn't miss the sadness in her eyes. There was something going on with her, and he was determined to get to the bottom of it after he got through the BBQ. Job sighed deeply before he headed off to pick up Anita.

Job and Anita spent over two hours in the grocery store. At one point, he thought she was going to purchase the entire store. They had two cart loads full. He loved her, but he made himself a promise right then and there that he'd never, ever go to the store with her again.

As they were leaving the store, two twin boys bump into their cart running by them. Job felt a pain in his chest as the tears welled up in his eyes.

He missed his family so much. Sometimes the silence was just too much for him to bear. Anita grabbed him and hugged him tightly as the boys, and their parents walked by looking at them curiously.

Anita forced Job to look at her. "Baby, I know this pain all too well. I have been where you are, losing your whole family like that can destroy you if you let it, but remember God never gives us more than we can handle. I know it may not seem like it, but I promise that you will get through this. I am telling you that from experience."

"When Michael went on to be with the Lord, I didn't know how I would survive alone after 40 years of marriage, but I knew I had to for Junior's sake. When I lost Junior not even seven months later, I felt so alone. I felt as if I had no one, but I had to trust God and keep pushing on.

"Baby there were many days that I didn't even want to get out of the bed. I just laid there calling on the Lord and begging him to take me home too. Then almost in the blink of an eye, God gave me you and your beautiful family. God gives us double for our trouble."

"I know we are never supposed to question God, but I can't help but wonder why? Why would he give me such a blessing and take it all away? Why my family? I never ever took them for granted. I don't understand Anita."

"At times, I wish that I was never born. If I had never been born, I would never have met Roni, and I would not have to endure this pain. I can't take this," Job cried. "It hurts so much." "I know baby," Anita cried. "Trust me I do, but we can't lean on our own understanding. Talk to Him, He always answers, not always the way we expect Him to, but He always answers."

As Job and Anita returned from the grocery store, a black truck with tinted windows pulled behind them in the driveway. Job smiled as his baby brother Carlos exited the driver's side first followed by his brothers Jonathan in the passenger seat and David in the back. "Wow little bro, you've been holding out on me. When did you get this?" Job asked, admiring the new truck. "Umm almost two weeks ago," Carlos stammered.

Job realized that he must have purchased the truck around the time of the accident which is why he didn't tell him. "I love this Carlos. You're making me want a new truck," Job smiled. "Thanks," Carlos beamed.

Job's approval means the world to him. "Where do you want us to put these ribs?" he asked as he started unloading the truck. "Just put them in the sink. I need to prep them now, so they will be ready by Saturday," Job answered.

Attached to the back of the truck is Jon's trailer with the largest charcoal smoker that Job and Anita had ever seen. "What in the world is that thing?" she asked. "I bought it for Job," Jon smiled. I saw it and knew that he'd love it. "Are you serious?" Job asked, admiring the massive smoker. "Yes, it's custom made, and it even has your initials engraved on the front." "Okay, you just officially became my favorite brother!" Job teased. "I love it, he said, hugging his brother.

They helped Job unload the groceries and the smoker from the trailer. "Did you leave anything at the store?" Jon laughed. "Barely, this woman can shop. Don't let the small frame fool you." Job laughed. "Yeah, I got your small frame," Anita said. "I can't wait until Saturday Job," Carlos said. "Me too and I'm going to find out your recipe one day," David added. Job smiled, unsure what God had planned for his life.

"Why don't you help me make it, that way you'll know how to do it right," Job smiled. "I have been asking you for this recipe for years. Let me check your forehead. You must be sick," David laughed. Job laughed off the comment. "I mean it is a family recipe." David looked at Job but decided not to press the issue. "Thanks Job, Chef BoyarDavid is in the house." Job laughed at his older brother, "Yeah okay, how about you try not burning the half smokes again?" he teased.

"No, see that was that off-brand charcoal Danielle bought," David disputed. "Besides, Tammy loved them." Everyone laughed. "Man, that girl loves you so much she would say anything. You could have grilled socks, and she would swear it tastes like steak," Carlos laughed.

"See you all are just jealous of my grill skills," David said, which made them all laugh. "That's okay baby," Anita smiled, "Come on in here and show me some of your potato peeling skills." David followed behind Anita, pouting while his brothers trailed behind teasing him.

# CHAPTER TWELVE

Job was up early Saturday morning praying. He asked God to give him wisdom on how to break the news to his family. Yesterday he called Mack and asked him to come to the BBQ. He told him his plan for breaking the news to his family and wanted him there to answer any questions that they may have. After praying, Job headed downstairs to put on his family famous ribs.

Of course, Anita was already awake. He could smell her green beans from his room. Job could not wait. "Anita you're doing it up in here?" Job smiled, inhaling the delicious aroma. I can smell the food all the way upstairs. Anita beamed, she loved for people to enjoy her meals. Anita did not believe in rushing to prepare a meal, and she refused to use the microwave for anything. "Don't you come in here sneaking anything either," Anita said. "Go put your ribs on and go for your run. I got my eyes on you Job."

Job couldn't help but laugh. She knew him all too well. "I have to run like this every day. If I didn't I'd be as big as a house eating your cooking every day," Job responded. Anita laughed and hugged Job. "It's so good to see you laugh Job," Anita smiled. It feels good to laugh," he said hugging her tightly. Job removed the ribs from the large refrigerator and took them outside and prepped them for his new smoker before starting out on his run.

When Job returned home, he showered, dressed and checked the ribs before heading to his office. It dawned on him during his run that he had not checked his messages in over a week. He decided that he could no longer avoid it. His voice-mail inbox at work and home have been full for days. There were several messages from his family and his friends Eli, Billy, and Alfonzo AKA Zo. He decided to call Zo first.

Before Job could say anything, Zo answered the phone, "Man I have left over ten messages for you, where have you been?" Zo demanded. "I know Zo, and I'm sorry man," Job apologized. "Things have just been crazy as you can imagine. I appreciate you checking in though." "It's good to hear your voice," Zo said. "We're going to have to go on one of our fishing trips again soon" Job smiled thinking about the last trip they took with their sons.

"Just let me know when and where," Zo said. "I'm looking for a reason to try out the new boat," Zo added.

"Cool, look I'm calling because I'm having a BBQ today. I know it's last minute but if you and Diane can make it we'd love to have you," Job said. "Okay, I know she'll be happy to see you. We've been praying for you man, and I'm always down for a BBQ, you need us to bring anything?" Zo asked.

"Nope, we've got everything covered. We're starting at 3:00, but you can come whenever," Job said as he went to check on his special sauce. "Cool, we'll be there. By the way, have you talked to Billy and Eli yet?" Zo asked. "Not yet, I'm going to call them when I hang up with you," Job said rubbing his head. "Okay, see you later man and thanks for everything," Job said. "That's what family is for," Zo smiled, hanging up the phone.

After Job hung up with Zo, he called Billy, Eli and Roni's family and invited them over as well. After making all his phone calls, Job was exhausted. He told Anita he wanted to take a short nap. "You okay baby?" Anita asked. "Yes, I'm fine. I didn't sleep much last night, and you know how the family likes to party, so I need to rest up." Job smiled. "You're right about that. Maybe I should take a nap too?" Anita laughed. "Ok, I will be back in an hour," Job said. I just checked the ribs, and the sauce is on a very low simmer, so they are fine." "Okay, call me if you need something," Anita said.

Job felt so much better after his nap. He showered again and changed before heading back downstairs. It was already 1:00. He hadn't planned to sleep so late. When he went downstairs, he noticed Anita's potato salad on the counter. He looked behind him to make sure that Anita wasn't around before he quietly removed a spoon from the drawer and took a heaping spoonful of potato salad. Just as he puts the spoon in his mouth, Anita walked in. All he could do is laugh and run out of the kitchen. "Job I'm gonna get you," Anita laughed and began chasing him. "If you don't keep yourself out of my kitchen!"

Job continued to laugh as he headed out to check on the ribs. They were coming along perfectly. He went into the kitchen to finish his sauce. Anita picked up her wooden spoon and glared at him as he entered the kitchen. "I'm just finishing the sauce," Job laughed. "Umm hmm, I'm watching you Job," Anita said. Job continued to laugh as he stirred his sauce.

Hey hey hey," they heard as the front door opened. Everyone knew it was Marcus before he entered the kitchen. "Hey Marcus," Job and Anita said. Marcus laughed as he and Leslie enter the kitchen. "How did y'all know it was me?" The others looked at each other and laughed.

Job walked over to hug his sister and brother. "Where's Michelle and the kids?" Job asked. Marcus and Leslie exchanged looks. "Umm I left Michelle home with them," Marcus replied looking at Leslie. Job looked at his brother with a puzzled stare. "Why?" he asked. "Well to be honest. I didn't want to make you uncomfortable Job," Marcus said nervously.

Job walked over to his brother. "Marcus you're my big brother, and I love you, but if you do not get my sis and nephews over here we are going have a problem," he said, and playfully put his brother in a choke hold. "I told him you were not going to be happy," Leslie said shaking her head.

"Okay, I will call her now," Marcus said, picking up the phone to call his wife. Job took the phone from him. "Hey Mimi," Job said. "Hey Job, is everything alright?" Michelle asked. "No, it's not, to be honest with you," Job said. "I want to know why you let my peanut head brother leave you and my nephews at home." Michelle laughed. "He thought it would be easier on you," she said. "I appreciate that," Job replied, "but there will be kids everywhere that I go and right now I need my family more than ever. All of them." "We're on our way," she smiled. "Thanks, sis," Job said hanging up the phone.

He playfully popped his brother on the back of his head. "Job, don't forget I'm bigger than you," Marcus said as Job laughed. "Yeah, but I'm wiser and faster," Job said. Anita laughed at the two of them. "Well, Mr. Fast and Wise you get over here and finish this sauce and Marcus go put that ice in the coolers before it melts all over my floor please."

# CHAPTER THIRTEEN

It wasn't long before people started arriving. Shortly before 3:00 Kim arrived, with two large pans and one small pan. "I made this one for you," Kim said as she handed Job the smaller pan. Job was grinning from ear to ear. "Okay, let me sneak this in the fridge, so no one else sees it." Leslie walked in the kitchen just as Job closed the refrigerator door.

He smiled and winked at Kim. "What is that about?" Leslie questioned, looking at her brother. "Oh, nothing sis," Job smiled. "You need something?" Job asked. "Yes, I still can't figure out how to work this dang-blasted intercom system," Leslie said.

Job shook his head as he put his arm around his sister's shoulder and showed her for the 10th time how to work the intercom system. A few minutes later, music was playing throughout the entire house. "How are you feeling?" Kim asked as Job reentered the kitchen. "I'm good," Job said. "I had a slight headache earlier, but I feel fine now." "Good, please try to take it easy today," Kim begged. "Yes ma'am," Job saluted sarcastically. "Very funny. How are you feeling about telling your family?" she asked softly.

"I'm just ready to get it over with, to be honest," Job sighed. "I'm also a little concerned about how they will take the news. These past two weeks has taken its toll on all of us. This situation isn't just about me, you know?" Kim nodded her head.

"I know it's going to be hard, but I believe that our faith will get us through it together, no matter what the outcome is, but trust me, I'm planning on being here for a long time," Job smiled. Kim hugged Job as she fought back her tears. "Don't you start crying," Job said. "You know I've always hated to see you cry," Kim smiled and nodded. "I know."

"We've got to catch up too," Job said. "I feel like we need to talk." Kim smiled. "I never could hide anything from you. Job you have a lot going on right now. We need to focus on you." "Kim, I need a distraction. There's so much going on that it would be so nice to not think of myself for once."

Kim nodded her head just as Eli, Billy, Zo and their wives entered the kitchen. There were immediate screams from the girls. They were the best of friends in high school, and while they had kept in touch via Facebook and Christmas cards during the years, they hadn't seen Kim in years.

"Okay, okay let us get in there too Kimmy," Eli said. "It's been forever." Kim smiled, "It has, how are you?" "I'm blessed," Eli smiled. "Girl you look good! That California life did you right!" Billy laughed, hugging Kim tightly. "Billy if you don't move out of the way and let me get my hug," Zo said. Hey Kim, it's so good to see you," Zo smiled. "You too Alfonzo. I like the bald head." Zo smiled rubbing his head. "Thank you, Kim."

Zo's wife Angie looked over at Kim and rolled her eyes, "Girl, please don't encourage him, he already thinks he's the next Michael Jordan." They hung around in the kitchen talking before heading to the sun-room. It felt like old times again.

Everyone that Job invited showed up. There was laughter all around as they reminisced about old times. As the evening started to wind down, Kim noticed Job sitting alone. "Are you okay?" she asked. "Yes, I'm just sitting here trying to figure out how to break this to them. They look so happy Kim."

"Job you don't have to do this today if you're not feeling up to it." "I know, but I want to put it behind me. No time like the present, right?" Job got everyone's attention. "I hope everyone is having a good time. I wanted to have this BBQ for several reasons. First, as a sincere thank you."

"The last couple of weeks have been horrifying for me, but I truly thank God for every one of you in this room. I know that without Him and you, I would not have made it this far." Job fought to hold in the tears that threatened to fall. "I am so grateful and blessed to have all of you in my life."

"I believe that God knew these things would happen long, long ago and sent you all to me for a time such as this. Words can't express how much I truly love you all." "We love you too baby," Angela said. Job smiled at her. "Now on to the other reason why I asked you all here," he said as he looked over at Mack.

"Earlier this week I was diagnosed with an inoperable brain tumor. Job paused to allow the news to sink in. Mack and his colleagues determined that this was the reason for the headaches I've been having the last few months.

They did not discover it sooner because it concealed itself behind a part of the brain that is hard to see unless you are looking for it."

Job's heart broke as he looked around the room. He saw the stunned expressions on the faces of his family and friends. The looked on his mother's face hurt him most. He took a deep breath before he continued. "Look guys, I need you now more than ever. I trust and believe that whatever happens is the Will of God, but I am not planning on going anywhere anytime soon, so I don't want anybody crying for me. I'm not sad or mad. If God does take me home it's just because Roni is up there complaining about taking care of the kids by herself," he joked.

There were a few chuckles as Roni always joked about divorce never being an option because she wouldn't allow Job to leave her to take care of the kids.

"Look no sad faces or tears, one way or another it's going to work out for God's glory and my good. Let's not think of the what-ifs and enjoy this moment we have right now, okay?" They all stood and hugged Job. "Let's pray," Marcus said as he put his arm around his brother's shoulder and wiped the tears from his eyes. After praying, everyone hugged Job again. "We're going to beat this," his sister

Adrienne said. Job smiled. "I love you," he said as he hugged her tightly.

"Look, I know that was not something you guys were expecting to hear when I invited you over, but I invited you all over to have a good time, and that's what we're going to do." "You're right Job. I'm going get this thing jumpin'," Carlos said. He moved some of the tables and chairs out of the way and switched the playlist. Job laughed and pulled Kim, Leslie and Anita to their feet as *"Before I Let Go" by Maze featuring Frankie Beverly* began echoing from the speakers.

# CHAPTER FOURTEEN

For the rest of the evening, no one thought about tumors or death. They just enjoyed the moment. The BBQ went into the wee hours of the morning. After the cleanup, everyone except Carlos headed home. Job looked at his brother as they took the last few bags of trash outside. "You okay baby bro?" Carlos dropped the bag and hugged his big brother. "No," he said into his brother's shoulder as he cried. Job put down his bag and hugged his brother back.

"Los it's okay," Job said. "It's not okay," he cried. "You don't deserve this. I'm not saying anybody does, but you don't. You are the most devoted man I know. If God can allow this to happen to you, I don't stand a chance." "Hold up Carlos, let me stop you right there. God doesn't owe me or anyone else anything."

"That's where we mess up. God gave us life. Everything after that is a gift. Don't ever stop trying to be a better man, a godly man. Look at my life, do you think I'd have any of this without God?" "What does it matter now?" Carlos cried. "You don't have your wife, kids and now you might die." Carlos shook his head and sat down on the sofa.

"First off, God isn't trying to hurt me, Carlos. I don't understand this either and to be honest, until we get to Heaven I probably never will. It's not meant for me to understand. We're supposed to trust Him. That's it, and that's all." "Job you know I love God," Carlos cried. "I think I learned to do that before I learned my ABCs, but it's hard. "Trust me Carlos, I know. This is not a walk in the park for me either.

I wake up some mornings wanting to scream and throw stuff, but that won't solve anything." Carlos fell to the ground and wept. "God please!" he cried. "Please don't take my brother from me. I will do anything. Take my life. I don't care, but please give him a break." Job knelt with his brother and hugged him tightly as they cried together.

The next morning Job decided to skip his usual morning run and Sunday services to spend the day with his baby brother. Job was drinking coffee and checking his email when his brother finally came downstairs. "Morning Job," Carlos said, not making eye contact with his brother.

Carlos looked like he hadn't slept all night. How are you feeling baby bro?" Job asked. "I'm okay," Carlos said quietly while pouring himself a cup of coffee. "I was thinking about taking the boat out and doing some fishing today. You have plans?" Job asked. "I do now," he smiled. Carlos hadn't been fishing since he went with their father the year before he died.

"Good, we can grab breakfast on the way," Job said. "Perfect because I am starving," Carlos said just as his stomach rumbled, agreeing with him. "I guess that makes three of us," Job laughed. "You mind driving? I want to ride in the new truck," Job said. Carlos smiled proudly, "Yeah I'll drive." "Cool," Job said. "Help me grab the stuff from the boathouse, and we can get on the road."

Job and Carlos enjoyed the ride to the Solomon's Island. Job didn't always have a lot of free time available, so he was enjoying spending this time with his baby brother. Carlos and Job discussed everything from Roni and the children to dating to Carlos' new promotion and him closing on his first home in two weeks.

"I'm proud of you," Job said. "Seriously, it's crazy; my little brother is a man." Carlos laughed, "I've been a man for a while now." Job laughed at him. "I know, but I still remember changing your diapers and here you are talking about buying a house. You make me feel old." "Well bro you are getting up there," Carlos laughed. "I prefer to think of myself as well- seasoned," Job laughed.

Their fishing trip was awesome. Job and Carlos caught a ton of fish. They end up giving some of it away to the other fishermen on the pier.

"Wow! I can't believe we gave away all that fish and we still have a lot left. What are you going to do with all these fish?" Carlos asked. "I think we should take it to the wharf and have it cleaned and have a fish fry next weekend," Job said. "Oh yeah, that would be perfect. Anita put a hurting on that fish last year," Carlos said. Job smiled. "I can taste it right now. I'll call Leslie and tell her to pass the word. Hey, did you know she's seeing someone?" Job asked.

Carlos smiled. "Yep she told me about him a couple of months ago, but she said she didn't want to say anything to the family until she knew for sure whether it was serious or not. I guess it is if she told you." "I guess so," Job sighed. He was extremely protective of his sister. Leslie had experienced more than her share of heartache in the past.

"Have you met this guy?" Job asked defensively. "I ran into them at Chart House a couple of months ago," Carlos said. "He seems like a good guy, and you can tell that he likes her a lot. He looked like a lovesick puppy. I gave him the Poppa Job stare though," Carlos laughed. Job laughed so hard he started to choke on the water he was drinking. "Man, Pop had that stare down," Job laughed. "Remember the first time he met Danielle's ex-boyfriend, Keith?" I thought Keith was going to pee on himself. Pops even felt sorry for him. I know, remember Danielle started crying." They both laughed so hard that Carlos had to pull over.

# CHAPTER FIFTEEN

When Job and Carlos got back to the house, the brothers put the freshly cleaned fish in the freezer and unloaded the truck. "Thanks for hanging out with me today," Job said. "We need to do this more often," he added. Carlos held back tears as he wondered how many more days like this he'd have with his brother. Job was close with all his siblings, but he shared a special bond with Leslie and Carlos.

Job could see the struggle in Carlos' eyes. "Okay little bro, you be safe," Job said as Carlos prepared to leave. Don't forget about the fish fry. "You know I won't," Carlos coughed, trying to hide the emotion in his voice. As Job walked back into the house, the telephone was ringing. "Hi Job, it's Kim. Can you come to the office tomorrow?" There have been a few developments. I'm not going to lie to you Job, it's bad." "Okay. I'll be there," he groaned.

There was an awkward silence on the phone. "Job I'm sorry. I hate being the bearer of bad news but I wanted to be the one to tell you." "I appreciate that," Job said. "Is there anything that I can do?" Job smiled at her kindness.

Kim had always been such a caring person. "Just pray," he said. "That's all we can do now." "If that ain't the truth," Kim said.

Job shook his head, "You sound just like your mom." Kim laughs. "Yeah, I've noticed more and more how I've picked up a lot of things from her." "She was such a sweet woman," Job said, "I miss her." "That makes two of us," Kim added as she smiled sadly holding back her tears. "You begin to put your life into perspective when you realize that your entire family is gone," before Kim finished she realized what she had said.

"Oh my God Job, I am so sorry. I didn't," Job interrupted her apology. "Kim, I know what you meant. Your mom was the only relative you had. I can't begin to understand how that feels but please don't ever think that you don't have a family because you will always have us." "Thank you, Job," Kim smiled.

"Well, I should be going. Call me if you need anything," Kim said. "Do you have plans for dinner?" Job asked. "Umm not really," Kim answered. "Not really? Hmm you have a date or something," he teased. "I sure do, with a Marie Callender frozen lasagna," she laughed.

"You better not ever let Anita hear you say that," Job laughed. He didn't hear Anita come in until she rounded the corner and entered the kitchen, "Hear who say what?" "Umm, I..I" Job stuttered, "Well," Anita held out her hand for the phone. "Hello?" "Hi Anita, it's Kim. How are you?" "I'm fine baby," Anita smiled. "Now what is Job talking about not letting me hear something." "Nothing really," Kim hesitated. "He asked about my dinner plans, and I told him I was going to fix a frozen lasagna."

"WHAT?!" Anita exclaimed. "I tried to warn you," Job yelled in the background. "Kim if you don't get yourself over here," Anita lectured. "Frozen lasagna...hmph...what in the world?" "Anita they are good. I will be fine," Kim tried to explain. "Dinner will be ready in 1 hour, we'll see you then," Anita said.

Kim realized that she would not win this battle. "Yes ma'am. Do you need me to bring anything?" Kim asked "Nothing, but your pretty little self. We have everything under control, okay?" Anita asked. "Yes ma'am, I will see you in an hour." "Good, drive carefully. Here's Job," Anita said handing the phone back to Job. "I tried to warn you," Job laughed. "I know, I know. Well, I guess I'd better turn the oven off and get ready," Kim laughed.

"Okay, see you in a bit," Job said. "Ok, bye," Kim laughed hanging up the phone.

Exactly one hour later Kim rang the doorbell. Job answered the door and led her to the kitchen. Anita was putting the last of the food on the table. "Oh my gosh, it smells amazing in here!" Kim gushed. Her mouth began to water at the delicious aroma. Anita smiled. "Thank you, baby. Frozen lasagna, um um um," Anita said, shaking her head. Kim and Job laughed. "Okay, I need to take Sister Jenkins a plate and sit with her for a bit. Do you need anything before I go?" Anita asked. "Nope, we're good," Job said, "Please give her my love." "I will baby," Anita said, heading out the door.

Kim stood to fix the plates when Job stopped her. "Please let me. People have been waiting on me and serving me hand and foot. I'd like to serve someone else." Kim smiled. "Sure." "Okay, we have ham, fried chicken, mac & cheese, sweet potatoes, fried cabbage, and cornbread. If you're nice to me, I might share some of my delicious banana pudding with you." Kim laughs. "Well, in that case, I promise to be very nice." Job and Kim laughed. "It's so good to see you laugh," Kim smiled. Job grinned as he continued fixing their plates.

As they ate Job decided that this was the perfect time to catch up with Kim. "So, what's been going on with you?" Job asked, reaching for a third helping of cornbread. "What do you mean?" Kim asked trying to evade the question. "Well you've been gone for a while, and we haven't talked since graduation," Job said. Kim laughed. "I guess we had to do this sooner or later huh?" "Yep so start at the beginning," Job said.

"Well, I ended up double majoring in forensic psychology and criminology. "I even wrote a couple of books which is how I ended up getting into the FBI." "Are you serious?" Job asked. "I'm impressed." "Yes, and thank you," she shyly smiled. I initially worked with them to help catch a few serial killers. I then joined the Crisis Management Unit. I had just been promoted to the head of the division when I met my husband, Gerald.

"He hated the idea of me working in such a dangerous unit." "I can understand that," Job agreed. "So, I ended up moving to the Behavioral Analysis Unit Division one year after my promotion where I did more behind the scenes work. I didn't like it as much, but I wanted to make him happy," she continued.

"Shortly after joining the unit, I started getting promoted. Gerald wasn't happy about that. A few months later I found out that I was pregnant and instead of him being excited, he was furious." Kim fought back her tears. "There were times when he'd come home and be so mean. I felt like Gerald hated me. He blamed me for getting pregnant even though he didn't want me taking birth control pills because it made me gain weight.

He never said he didn't want children. In retrospect, I probably should've asked him, but I assumed those were things you would volunteer during the dating period before you discuss getting engaged, let alone get married. It's like he was jealous of the baby." Job listened intently.

He couldn't imagine being jealous of a baby. He always thought of his children as blessings. "Anyway, my pregnancy was high-risk, so they put me on bed rest and told me that I had to refrain from certain wifely duties. That made Gerald so angry. One night he came home drunk and forced himself on me. I tried as best I could to stop him, but Gerald was stronger. He hit me and told me that if I didn't stop, he would kill the baby and me, so I just laid there and cried silently. When it was over, I felt relieved and dirty if that makes any sense."

Job nodded as he tried to keep his anger in check. Kim was the sweetest person in the world. There was once a time when he thought she would be the mother of his children. The fact that this punk hurt her because she was carrying his child was mind-boggling and made Job sick to his stomach. "So later that night I started to bleed," Kim continued. "I repeatedly prayed as I dressed to drive myself to the hospital. He stopped me and told me the baby was probably already dead anyway."

"He tore off my clothes and forced me to sleep with him again. In some sick and twisted way, I think he enjoyed it more because he knew he was hurting me." Job got up from his seat and sat next to her and handed her a tissue to wipe her eyes. "After he fell asleep, I left and went to the ER. I knew that my baby was already gone. I just felt it." Kim paused as she began to cry. "I had never felt so alone in my life."

"I wouldn't dare tell my mom about it. I didn't want her to worry about me although I get the feeling that she knew something wasn't right. From that moment on he continued to abuse me for the next two years, and I had three more miscarriages during that time. "He told me that he'd kill me if I ever left him and I believed that he would." "I'm so sorry you had to go through that," Job said trying to contain his anger and console her at the same time. "I wish I had known what was going on," Job murmured.

"I'm glad you didn't. You probably would've done something crazy," Kim said. "Maybe you're right." "How did you end up getting away?" Job asked. "Well the night I found out my mom died we were out celebrating our anniversary with his family and friends." "Needless to say, when I got the call I was distraught. Gerald was angrier than I'd ever seen before."

"When we got home, he nearly beat me to death because I had ruined his evening. He told me that he would not allow me to attend my mom's funeral because I needed to be home taking care of him and he wasn't going to the funeral."

"Can you believe this man told me to let the state bury my mother? That was the straw that broke the camel's back. One of his friends knew what is going on. He planned for Gerald to go to Vegas with him a few days later. I finally got the courage to tell my boss what is going on when I went to quit. He pulled some strings and was able to have me transferred here. I filed for divorce a week after moving back, and I've been here since."

"Wow, that's quite a life you have led Ms. Godwin," Job smiled sadly, hugging her. "It really has been, but overall there isn't a lot that I would change," Kim said. "Mom always said, crisis builds character. I've got a lot of character."

"So, where you are you staying now?" Job asked. "I know your mom was in hospice after she sold the house." "I'm renting a house in DC for the moment," Kim said. "Well if you ever need a change of scenery we have plenty of room here, and you are always welcome," Job said.

Kim suddenly became quiet. What is it?" Job asked. "Job I really shouldn't be telling you this, and I could lose my job if anyone found out that I told you, but I can't allow you to go in there blindsided tomorrow," Kim said. "Talk to me Kim," Job pleaded.

"While the investigation did prove that you're innocent, Samuel Jacobson bankrupted your entire company, and your employees' retirement plans have been depleted. "How is this possible? My God," he said. "They covered their tracks very well, but luckily your auditor knew what to look for and followed the trail. They've all been arrested and given statements except Samuel," Kim assured him. "I can't believe this," Job said.

"These people depended on me, and I failed them. What do I tell them now?" "I honestly don't know Job, but I can tell you this, you didn't fail anyone. You did the best that you could. Samuel Jacobson and the others failed them. Tomorrow they are going to announce that you've been cleared and release the hold on your accounts if that gives you any comfort at all." Job shook his head. "I am so concerned about my staff. They have families. Lord, please give me the wisdom to fix this," Job prayed.

# CHAPTER SIXTEEN

The next morning as Job returned from his morning jog he thanked God for wisdom. Job knew what he had to do because it's the right thing. Job headed out to meet with Kim and Agents Williams and Benavidez. "Mr. Arrington, you've been in my prayers," Agent Williams smiled when Job and his lawyers entered the office. "Thank you, Agent Williams," Job said shaking the older man's hand.

"Right this way," he said as he led the group down the hall to the small conference room. "Mr. Arrington, we've concluded our investigation, and we're confident that you were not involved. We're also releasing statements to various news sources absolving you of any guilt. Unfortunately, your company has suffered a significant financial blow.

Here are the details," Agent Williams said handing folders over to Job and his attorneys. Job closed his eyes after reviewing the contents. "Mr. Arrington I'm sorry again for your losses," Agent Williams said before exiting the room. "Thank you for everything," Job said. "And thank you too," Job said, turning to Kim. "I don't know what I would've done without you.

I had Leslie set up a meeting tomorrow with my staff. I want to be completely honest with them and let them know what's going on. I have prayed about it and decided to sell the bulk of my stock portfolio and close out most of my retirement accounts and give the money to my staff." "Wow! Job, you are such a good man," Kim said.

"I'm a man who trusted the wrong people and these people should not have to pay for my mistake. I don't know what Samuel was thinking," Job said. "We've worked alongside these people for years. We've been through everything together."

"Job, I know it's easy for me to say but you can blame yourself all day long, but the fact is that this could've happened to anyone. You put all the necessary precautionary measures in place to ensure there were no discrepancies. This situation is an anomaly." "When have you ever heard of an entire accounting department charged with fraud? You did the right thing. Samuel and his team let them down, not you. You have to understand that," Kim said.

"My head knows that, but all my heart keeps thinking about all the innocent people that will be financially ruined by this." "Of course," you're a decent person Job. "Anyone would feel that way in your position." Job was about to respond when his cell phone rang.

"Excuse me for a minute Kim," "Hello mother," Job said into his cell phone. Job looked at Kim and shrugged. She mouthed to him that she would be right back. Job nodded as she exited the room. "Is everything okay Mom?" "Yes, we haven't talked in the last week, and I just wanted to check on you."

"Everything is going as well as can be expected, mom. I did get one piece of good news though. The investigation is over, and they were able to prove that I was innocent," Job said. "I knew that," Angela smiled proudly. It's good that they made it official though. So when will you be getting back to work?" "Well that's the thing mother," Job sighed. "The company is now bankrupt, so there is nothing to get back to," Job said. "Job, I'm so sorry. You can see now why I don't waste my time praying," Angela commented. "Mother, please not today," Job pleaded. "Job I am sorry, sweetie I didn't call to argue. I am just stating the facts.

Where did serving God get your father Job? He was the most faithful man I have ever known, but I watched that faithful man suffer for years," she cried. "Why would a God of mercy allow someone who loved Him and was so devoted to Him to suffer like that Job? Why would He strike my first born with a tumor and try to take him from me too? When I think about those beautiful babies" she cried. "If I were you I would just be done with that whole God mess." "MOTHER!" Job demanded.

Job paused and took a deep breath before continuing, as his head began to pound. Job did not want to say something to his mother that he would end up regretting. "Mother I don't know why this is happening, but I do know that dad would be so hurt to hear you speak this way. I know it hurts but God's grace is the only reason why I am still able to stand. His mercy is what gets me through each day." Angela closed her eyes trying to shut out Job's words.

"Mother I once heard Pastor Miles say that Christians are like teabags without labels and the only way to tell what type of Christian they are is to put them in hot water. Mom I assure you, it gets no hotter than this, but I'll never forsake God because He has never forsaken me. I don't know why God took them and there's not one day that goes by that I don't think of them, but it gives me comfort knowing that dad continued to praise over his pain. I know he'd tell me to do the same thing.

I push forward thinking of him playing with my children in Heaven, free from all pain mother." "Job, you are my son, and I love you. I know we have not seen eye to eye a lot lately, but I need you to know that I love you more than you could begin to imagine."

"Mother that has never, ever been a question in my mind. I know you love me, just like I know you still love the Lord." Angela did not respond to his last statement. "Are you taking your medication?" she asked, changing the subject. "Yes mother," Job said. It helps a lot with the pain, but there isn't anything else he can give me." Angela closed her eyes, fighting back her tears. The thought of losing her son was too much for her to bear.

"I want to spend some time alone with you," Angela said. "We haven't done that since your father..well I think it's just long overdue." "I agree mother," Job smiled. "I'm meeting with the staff tomorrow to go over everything. How about we have lunch after?" Job suggested. Angela smiled. "That sounds nice. Would you mind if I cooked? I'm not really in a mood to go out." "Absolutely mother,"

Job said. "I love you, baby," Angela smiled. "I know mother, and I love you more. I'll see you tomorrow at noon."

# CHAPTER SEVENTEEN

After Job hung up the phone, he reached for his medication. His head was throbbing. Kim was walking in the room when she noticed Job grab his head. "Job are you okay?" she asked. "I'm fine Kim," Job smiled trying to ease her fears. "Just a little headache," he said. Kim held back her tears. Although she and Job had been out of contact for years, he would always be the love of her life. She had never loved any man the way she loved him including Gerald. Job noticed her tears and hugged her. "Kimmy, I promise you, it's going be okay," Job said.

Kim was a devout Christian, and she trusted God wholly, but she felt like her trust has been tested more than ever the last few years. She could only imagine how Job was feeling. She knew that this was a test of faith that she'd have to pass to fully support Job. "I know," Kim nodded. "Everything will work out the way it's meant to work out." "That it will," Job smiled.

"Want to grab lunch?" "Sure, but I'm getting a salad," Kim said. "I know I've gained at least 20 pounds the last two weeks," Kim laughed, wiping her eyes. Job laughed. "I know, now you see why I exercise so much. How about that place in Old Town with those chicken pita salads?" "Yes! I forgot all about that place."

Half an hour later, Kim and Job arrived at the waterfront in Alexandria, VA. "Wow, I have missed this place!" Kim said looking out at the water. Places like this remind me how much I missed home. "There's no place like home," Job said. "Okay Dorothy," Kim laughed. "Hey, I love that movie. I'm serious though," Job said.

"A couple of times Roni and I toyed with the idea of moving down south, but I love the DMV. We have such a rich history that gets overshadowed by politics a lot of the time. That's why my business had to be based here. I was adamant about that." "Well, I am glad you stayed," Kim smiled. "Me too.

"By the way, I've wanted to get your opinion about something." "Sure, what is it?" Kim asked. "Well as you know, Angel's best friend was also on the plane," Job says. Kim nodded. "I've been trying to reach out to her mom since the accident, and she has shut me down every time," Job explained. "We were on pretty good terms before this happened. I'm just looking for some advice on how to deal with her. I don't want to be pushy, but I want to express my condolences properly."

"Ashleigh was her only child, and she was raising her alone. In some ways, I feel her pain may be greater than mine. It was only the two of them for so long. She doesn't have any family here which is why they gravitated to us. She's a nice person, but she's filled with so much bitterness."

"She has this constant woe is me attitude." Kim nodded. "I know a lot of women like that," Kim said. "Job, you're a kind-hearted person. I know you want to make sure she's okay, but she may need a little time. I know that's not the answer you want to hear, but you don't want to come off as intrusive."

"Sometimes when people are hurting they don't have a clear perception of things. Just give her some time, she'll come around." "You're right. I will be patient," Job nodded. "When did you last contact her?" Kim asked.

"I sent money for the funeral and flowers the day after the funeral with a card." "I wanted to attend the funeral, but it was private, so I asked her to contact me if she needed anything and that I look forward to talking to her soon." "Good, that's perfect," Kim smiled. "That leaves the ball in her court."

"I just feel like she blames me," Job said. "Job please don't go down that road again. You know how the enemy tries to play mind games. Look at me," Kim said. Job looked into her eyes as tears fell down his face. "Job this is not your fault. Do you hear me?" Kim said, rubbing Job's arm as he wiped away his tears. "I just wish she knew how much we loved Ashleigh."

"I'm sure that she does know. She's probably in a lot of pain right now," Kim said. In my heart, I know it's not my fault, but I don't know I'm just tired I guess," Job said. "Ahhh ya think?" Kim asked laughing. Job smiled. "Job you have through hell," she said. "You need some time. I'm sure you'd look awesome in the uniform, but you are not superman." Job laughed.

"Thank you so much, Kim. You have been such a blessing to my life. I hope you know how much I appreciate you being here for me." Kim rubbed Job's hand. "You would've done the same for me. As you said, we're family. Speaking of, how is everyone doing?" Kim asked.

"They are getting better. I had an interesting conversation with my mom earlier. It didn't start off great, but in the end, she invited me over for lunch tomorrow," Job said surprised. "That is awesome Job," Kim smiled. "I love her so much Kim," Job said. "She's just become so bitter since dad died.

The funeral was her first time at the church since dad's funeral. I know she still loves God, but she cannot see past her anger, and I can't allow that spirit to come on me." Kim nodded her head. "I didn't realize your mom had stopped going to church. She's the main reason my mom and I started going to church," Kim said. "Yep, she blames God for allowing my father to die," Job said shaking his head. "Can I be honest with you?" Job asked. "Always," Kim said.

It frustrates me so much when people keep commenting on how well I am holding up. They have no idea what I go through at night, but it's like with my children. I have always taught them that we nor the world owe them anything. Whatever we choose to give you, we also have the power to take away from you. I'm no different than any other man. I struggle daily, but I make a conscious choice to trust God, and I'm not going to lie it has been a hard choice to make the last few weeks."

"To whom much is given, much is required," Kim said. "People admire you Job, but I'm sure it can be a bit much sometimes. It's easy for someone to look at your life and say you have it made, but they only see a snapshot, not the full picture." "Exactly," Job agreed. "We cannot expect to conquer without conflict. I feel guilty when I feel overwhelmed. I'm in no way comparing myself to Jesus, but we're supposed to be Christ-like, and Jesus never complained. He just dealt with it without ever complaining."

"That's why He is the only perfect son Job. You are a supernatural being living in a natural world. You're going to get tired sometimes. There is nothing wrong with that. God never said He wouldn't give us anything to complain about, He said he'd give us the strength to make it through, and you're doing that. Every single day that you get out of bed and praise Him despite your pain, you're doing that."

# CHAPTER EIGHTEEN

Job dropped Kim back off at her office a short time later before heading home. As he turned into his driveway, a strange woman attempted to approach his car before Sean blocked her path. "Are you Jobias Arrington?" the woman asked looking around Sean. "It's okay guys, yes I'm Jobias Arrington, how may I help you?" he asked cautiously.

"Good, this is for you sir," she said as she handed him an envelope and walked away. "Have a good day," the woman said before reentering the car waiting nearby. Job thanked Sean and drove up to the house. Job sat in the car for the next 10 minutes, staring the court summons. He could not believe that Ashleigh's mother was suing him.

Job leaned his head back on the headrest and closed his eyes. He suddenly felt as if he's going to be sick. Job jumped when Sean tapped on the window. "Job, I'm so sorry," Sean apologized. "I didn't mean to scare you. Tim noticed that you still hadn't gotten out of the car and wanted to make sure you were okay." "Yes, I'm fine. Thank you." "Okay, let me know if you need anything Job," Sean said. "Thanks, Sean and thank Tim for his concern." "Sure thing Job," Sean said before walking back to his post.

Job entered the house and headed to the kitchen, following his friend's voices. Eli, Billy, and Zo were sitting at the table eating and waiting for him. They looked up as he entered the kitchen. "Hey old man," Zo said. "What are you guys doing here besides eating up all my food," Job laughed. "We just wanted to drop by to make sure that you're okay," Billy said, hugging his longtime friend. "we saw the news report," Eli said. "Congrats Job, I know it feels good to have all that behind you," Zo said as he places his plate in the sink and kissed Anita on the cheek.

"It does feel good, but Samuel drained the company. It looks like I'm going to have to shut down. I'm meeting with the staff tomorrow to let everyone know," Job said solemnly. "That reminds me I need to call Leslie; can you give me a minute?" Job asked. "Sure Job, take your time," Eli said.

Job went to his office to call Leslie. "Hey Job," she answered, "Is everything okay"? "Well yes and no," he responded. "The good news is that the investigators have cleared me of any wrong-doing. The bad news is that Samuel and his people completely wiped the company out." "Oh my gosh Job. No," Leslie cried. "I want to meet with everyone tomorrow to let them know what's going on. No sense in delaying it," Job sighed. "I guess you're right." "How are you holding up?" his sister asked.

"I have been better, but I'm not going to cry over spilled milk," Job said. "Okay, well I will email everyone and let them know we're meeting tomorrow. What time?" Leslie asked. "Let's shoot for 10:00 AM," Job said. "Got it and I'm so sorry Job. I know how much the company meant to you," Leslie said. "Thanks Sis, I love you," Job said. "Eli and the guys are here so let me get back to them. I will call you later." "Okay Job, I love you more," Leslie said, hanging up the phone.

Job entered the family room and sat next to Eli on the sofa. "So, as I was pulling into the driveway just now, I received this," he said passing the summons around. "I need to call Matt," Job said rubbing his temples. Anita walked in carrying a pitcher of her famous peach iced tea. "Call Matt for what?" she asked. "Theresa is suing me for the wrongful death of Ashleigh," Job said as his voice cracked. "That's the craziest thing I've ever heard. You and Roni were better parents to that baby than she ever was," Anita responded.

"I'm going to keep her in prayer," Anita said as she placed the pitcher on the table, "Lord knows she needs all she can get. Do you need anything else?" she asked. "No, this is fine Anita, thanks," Job said, pouring himself a glass of tea. "So how much is she after?" Billy asked. "100 million dollars." "WHAT?!" Billy choked. "Well despite all of this, have you been holding up okay?" Zo asked. "I'm not going to lie, Zo, it's hard, but with God's grace, I will get through this," Job said. "I never in a million years thought I would be in this position. I thought Roni and I would grow old together" Job said fighting back his tears.

Zo and Billy looked at each other awkwardly. "What?" Job asked. "Well I need you to receive what I'm about to say in love," Billy said. "I'm listening," Job said cautiously. "Well we've been talking, and we came to the same result that perhaps God is trying to get your attention." "Well, He has done that," Job laughed sadly. Zo sat across from Job continuing, "I mean the company, your family, the tumor, and now Ashley's mom is suing you. All of this seems like way too much of a coincidence Job. I'm just saying maybe you need to seek God and ask him to reveal if there is anything that you have done that may have played a part in all of this."

Job looked at Zo like he had two heads. He felt like he was in the twilight zone. "You don't think I've done that a thousand times already Zo?" Job questioned. "Every second of every day I wonder why God chose to take my family and leave me. Is this why you all came here? To condemn me?" Job asked looking at each of them. Eli and Billy's guilty expressions told him that they agreed with Zo. "Job no one is condemning you, but you have to explore the possibility that maybe you inadvertently contributed to these things and maybe this is your punishment," Billy explained. Job shook his head.

"Either this is the worst joke ever, or you have seriously lost your minds," Job said in disbelief. "Maybe it's not all about you at all Job. Who knows? What if perhaps it's Roni? I mean no disrespect Job, but she wasn't even a Christian until she met you so who knows what went on in her past or her families' past," Billy said in an ill-fated attempt to defend Job. "Job look we're here because we love you," Zo said. "We can't sit by and act like we don't see this happening. We only want to help," Zo continued.

"Wow is this your way of helping me Zo?" Job asked. "You come into my home and question my character and my integrity. You have known me since we were kids.

What is it that you think I could've done that would cause my entire family to have to suffer the consequences?" You blame my family," Job cried. "And speak ill of my wife. I cannot believe that this is happening. You guys are supposed to be my friends, my family," Job cried. "We are your family Job," Eli said. "If we didn't love you we would not be here right now. The truth is not always easy to hear Job."

"You guys are no better than the people in these tabloids," Job remarked angrily. "Speaking on what you think. My life is my sermon. I am far from a perfect man, and I've made my share of mistakes, but I have done nothing that would cause my entire family to be destroyed." "Job look we didn't come here to offend you or have you offend us," Zo replied. "Offend you? You cannot be serious. You know what? Since you think I'm so tainted and God is punishing me for all the sins you think I'm committing why don't you leave?" "Come on Job we've been friends too long. We all care about you," Zo said.

"You have a funny way of showing it," Job retorted. "With everything else that I have to deal with you bring this to me now. I come and tell you another stone has been thrown, and you come in here and throw three more," Job said. "Job if this were happening to anyone else, wouldn't you feel that God was trying to get their attention?" Eli asked. "I would feel like that person needed my prayer and compassion Eli, not my judgment. I also hope and pray that before I had the slightest inclination to judge them for whatever imperfections I think that they may have, I would have empathy and realize there but for the grace of God, go I," Job added.

"I've known you all since we were still in pampers. I cannot believe this is happening." "Do you even know me? Did you know my family? You never once said hey man we're here to pray for you and stand with you. You go way out in left field. What happened to praying for someone? It's funny how you guys thought I was fine until all of this started happening. So, tell me what exactly do you think I've been doing? I'm sure you have some theories." "Job look we understand how you feel," Billy said trying to calm things down.

"Really? Do you?" Job questioned. "So, you just had your entire family taken from you in the blink of an eye, Billy? You've had every single part of your life completely change overnight right? Right?" Job angrily demanded. Billy silently looked away from Job. "Exactly," Job said in anger. "You have no idea how I feel. Every morning you get up and go to work and when you come home your children run to the door to greet you. You lay next to your wife at night," Job said as he began to cry."

"Every day, since I was a teenager I've asked God to remove anything from me that would cause me to sin against him," Job cried. "I did everything I knew to do, and that still wasn't enough, yet you sit here judging me. Maybe I did unknowingly offend God because I would be lying if I told you that I didn't internally wonder why my family. There are evil people in this world who rape and murder without rhyme or reason yet they live, their families live. I've wondered why He chose to take them instead of me. Maybe that is my sin" Job said.

He looked around the room at his friends as they sat in complete shock. They hadn't expected Job to react this way. He had always been a quiet and mild-mannered man. Job shook his head in disbelief. "You need to leave my house right now," he said calmly. "Job, come on man," Zo pleaded. "Look maybe we didn't go about this the right way," Zo said looking at Billy and Eli, "but we are family Job. Everything that's happened has proven that tomorrow is not promised to any of us. We can't leave things like this." "Zo, I appreciate that, but right now any attempt made would not be genuine.

I must forgive you if I want God to forgive me but unless God performs a miracle. I cannot forget this. You were my brothers, and I love each one of you unconditionally, but our season is over," Job said. "In a million years, I would've never expected this from you," Job said looking around at his friends. "I thought if anyone had my back. It would be you.

To have you come into my home and tell me that my wife and I are the reasons why this is happening," Job shook his head. "I don't even have words to describe how I feel right now," Job said. "I cannot believe you would do something like this." "Job sometimes the truth is hard to hear, but in truth there is healing," Eli retorted. "Who's truth, Eli?" Job asked.

"What happened to judge not lest ye be judged? You weren't so holier than thou when you got your assistant pregnant not once, but twice were you? And Billy do you know man times my wife prayed with your wife to keep her from leaving you after you gambled away your entire savings. And Zo, did I ever once condemn you when you fell off the wagon and started drugging again? No, instead of coming to any of you and judging you, I took it to God. I prayed for you and in many cases with you.

I would never have treated any of you the way you just treated me, but like I was telling Mother earlier today. You know a Christian by how they act when the heat comes. Thank you for showing me who you truly are. Trust and believe that I love you and I will continue to pray for you, but I can't have you in my life," Job said. "Do what you have to do brother. I wish you the best," Eli said storming out of the room. "Come on Zo," Billy said following Eli without looking back.

Zo nervously walked over to Job with tears in his eyes. "I'm sorry Job." I truly am." Job sat on the couch as the door closed behind Zo. Job rubbed his temples as he tried to control the pounding in his head, praying that the pain would subside soon. Anita entered the room and sat next to him, handing him a glass of water and two of his pills. "Thank you, Anita."

"I guess you heard huh?" Job asked. "I did," she said quietly. "I'm so proud of you Job. You stood your ground." "Is that really what people think about me?" Job cried. "Listen don't you pay attention to what people say about you. Let them talk," Anita said. "Easier said than done," Job frowned. "I don't want to bring shame on my family, and we both know the last thing we need is another scandal."

"There are enough negative perceptions of Christianity. I don't want to be one of them," Job said. Anita pointed at the dining room table. "Job, there are more than 200 cards on that table from people who love and support you. Read them, and you'll see just how most people view you. Dinner is ready whenever you are," she said as she rubbed his back. "Okay, thanks Anita. I'm not hungry right now. I think I will read some of these cards. I need to send thank you cards too. I'm already on top of it," Anita said. Job smiles. "What would I do without you, Anita?" Job asked. "Well let's hope you never have to find out," she laughed to herself.

Anita hugged Job and kissed him on the cheek. She knew how much he hurt and it was so hard for her to sit back and listen to Eli, Billy and Zo speak to Job that way. They were the first ones running to him for money and had the nerve to treat him that way. She knew that their accusations hurt Job and prayed that the Lord would comfort him.

# CHAPTER NINETEEN

Job's spirits were immediately lifted after going through a few of the sympathy cards from his children's classmates. There was such an outpouring of love for his family. There were cards from his college friends, professors and even a few friends he had met in summer camp that he'd stayed in contact with throughout the years.

Job cried tears of joy as he realized how much his family meant to people. Job was down to the last few cards when he noticed one post-marked from Oman. Job's heart began to pound as he took a deep breath before opening the card.

*Job-*

*Words cannot begin to describe the pain I felt at hearing of your devastating loss. As I write this, tears fall from my eyes. There has been an indescribable pain that I've felt since hearing about this tragedy. Roni and the kids were always so kind to me. You all were the family that I never had. I need you to know that this was never personal Job. I know you won't believe me, but I love you. I thought I'd have the money back to you before you ever noticed anything. The gambling just got out of control, and before I knew it I was making one horrible decision after another, but I didn't feel like I had any other option. It's crazy how you find yourself doing things that you never thought you'd do in a million years. When I truly realized the impact of what I had done it was already too late. I am so sorry that on top of all of this, you have to endure everything that my disloyalty has caused. Please know that you are and will always remain my brother. I never meant to hurt you. I sent everything that I have incriminating myself to the FBI, but please know that I'll never return to the states. I cannot go to jail Job. I hope that this will be over for you soon. I ask for your forgiveness, which knowing you, you've already extended. Job you're a good man, and I never deserved your friendship or your trust. I am sorry for everything. You are in my prayers.*

*-SAJ*

Job felt numb after reading the words. He was so engrossed in the letter that he didn't notice Anita standing over him with his dinner. "Job it's almost 10:00, you need to eat." She noticed the look on Job's face. "Is everything okay?" He handed her the letter. Anita sat down next to Job. "How do you feel?" Anita asked after reading the letter. "Honestly Anita, stupid because I feel sorry for him.

I have to go tell 150 people that they no longer have a job tomorrow because of him, but here I am feeling sorry for him like he's the victim."

"Job, he is a victim. Anyone who allows the enemy to use them is a victim until they become victorious over that which keeps them in bondage. He needs your prayers now more than ever. Samuel is not a bad person. He just allowed the sin of greed to overtake him." Job shook his head. "I know you're right. You think it's too late for me to call Kim?" Job asked. "No," Anita said, "You know you young folk are night owls."

"Young folk huh?" Job laughed, looking down at his plate. "Oh my goodness," Job said. "Is that smothered chicken, mashed potatoes and your famous skillet corn?" Job asked with a huge smile. Job blessed his food and began to devour it. Anita loved to watch him eat. "I'm going to head to bed unless you need anything else," she said. "Nope, I'm good Anita."

Job stood up from the table and hugged her. "Thank you for everything. I know God put you in our lives for a reason. You are like a second mother to me. I love you so much," Job said with tears in his eyes. Anita started tearing up. She lightly pats his arm. "Stop before you make me cry," Anita said, handing Job the phone. Job smiled.

He loved Anita more than words could say and thanked God for bringing her into his life. Job woke up earlier than usual the next morning and went through his usual morning routine. On the way to the office, he prayed that God would grant him favor. The last thing he wanted was for his employees to hate him.

Job was happy that he had decided to arrive at the office early. His nerves were starting to get to him. His cell phone rang as soon as he finished praying. "Hey Kim, how are you?" he asked. "I've been better," Kim said. Job noticed that Kim didn't sound like herself. "Kim is everything okay?" Job asked with concern in his voice. "I called last night, but didn't get an answer." "I know. I'm sorry Job," Kim says.

"Gerald showed up last night. I'm don't even know how he found me." "Are you okay? Did he hurt you?" Job asked. "Yes, I'm okay, and no, he didn't hurt me. I called the police immediately," Kim said trying to calm Job's nerves. The last thing she wanted to do it worry him. "He gave me some speech about how he's been going to counseling, and he's a changed man. He even said that I'm going against God's Will if I divorce him."

"Do you agree with him?" Job asked. "No, I'll never go back," Kim said. "I begged him to sign the papers and let me go. He doesn't love me. He just looks at me like his property. He wants to own me." "Do you think he'll sign the papers?" Job asked. "Not unless he's forced to do so," Kim said forcing back tears. "He told me that he was trying to be a gentleman and I'm his wife until death do us part.

"Where are you?" Job demanded as he started his truck. "I'm on my way." "No Job I am fine really," Kim assured him. "I hate the thought of this guy knowing where you live Kim," Job explained. "You can't go back there," I'm not staying," Kim promised. "There is an officer with me; I just came here to get my things. I'm packing up everything now."

"I would love it if you'd come to stay with Anita and me," Job said. "We have plenty of room and that way we can all rest knowing that you are safe." "Job that is a very generous offer, but I cannot do that," Kim replied. "You can, and you will," Job said. "Look I have to meet with my staff in an hour. While you are packing, I'm going to have Sean come to help you. Will you need a moving truck?" "No, I only have a few suitcases," Kim said.

"Okay, text me the address, and I will send it to Sean," Job said. Kim was quiet for so long that Job thought the call had disconnected. "Hello, Kim are you there?" Job asked. Kim sniffed into the phone. "Job you don't have to do this. You have enough on your plate without adding me and my problems to the list." "Kim, I do have to do this. If not, I'm going to constantly be wondering whether you're safe or if he's following you. If you truly don't want me to worry, then come to stay with us. At least until we figure out how to get this guy out of your life permanently."

"Thank you, Job," Kim sighed. "I appreciate everything that you've done for me. I insist on paying you rent," Kim said defiantly. "Kim don't make me jump through this phone," he said. "Job you cannot expect me to live off you guys. I have to pay my way please," Kim pleaded.

"How about you help Anita with the cooking? That will be payment enough," Job said. "You drive a hard bargain Mr. Arrington," Kim smiled into the phone. "You should know that Ms. Godwin," Job said, relieved that Kim decided to take him up on his offer. So, are you all set for the meeting?" she asked.

"I think so," Job said. "I'm just praying that they'll forgive me for allowing this to happen. "What are you doing for the rest of the day?" Job asked, wanting to change the subject. "I'm off today. I had planned on looking for a new place, but since that's out I'm not sure," Kim laughed. "Okay, I'll be home after lunch with my mom." "I think that'll be good for both of you," Kim said. Me too," Job agrees.

"How about we all go see a movie later?" Job suggested. "That sounds like fun. I haven't been to the movies in ages, but I'll only go if you allow me to treat everyone to dinner also," Kim added. "Perfect, I'll have a porterhouse steak and most expensive lobster on the menu," Job teased. "Whatever," Kim laughed.

"Well, I know you have things to do so I will let you get to it. I'll be praying for you Job. "Thank you so much Kim, I'll see you shortly," Job said. After Job ended his call with Kim, he walked toward the building and looked around at everything he'd worked so hard to obtain. He couldn't believe it was over. "Lord I don't know what you have planned for my life, but I know there is a purpose in everything. Amid all this confusion, I trust you," Job prayed.

As Job entered the building, he noticed one of his security officers sitting at the front desk. "Jamal, what are you doing here? The meeting isn't for another hour." "Old habits die hard," Jamal laughed. Jamal was a smart young guy who had gotten caught dealing drugs when he was a teenager. He was arrested at 18 and served ten years. He was arrested when his girlfriend was eight months pregnant and had never even held his son. Job met him during one of the prison ministry outings and took an instant liking to him. Job told him that if he were serious and wanted to get his life together, he'd have a job waiting for him the day he came home. Jamal was true to his word.

He showed up on the day he was released, still wearing his prison blues. He was a hard worker and worked his way up from the mail room to one of his top security officers. Job had a lot of respect for him. His ex-girlfriend was killed while Jamal was in prison. His son who was five at the time of his mother's death witnessed the entire thing.

Jamal's mom took custody of the boy and raised him until Jamal came home. His son started getting into trouble before he came home. Jamal was determined to do whatever he had to do to ensure that his son did not follow in his footsteps. Jamal eventually gained his son's love and respect, and he was now a model father and husband.

"What time did you get in?" Job asked. "6:00"," Jamal said as Job smiled, shaking his head. "By the way, thank you so much for coming to the funeral service. I appreciated it," Job said. "No doubt Job," Jamal said. "I didn't know your family well, but they were always nice and treated me with respect whenever I saw them." "Thanks Jamal," he smiled. "So, it's bad huh?" Jamal asked, looking around the lobby." "I'm not going to lie to you Jamal. It's as bad as it gets."

"I am so sorry. I feel like I let everybody down," Job said. "Job, rumors have been flying since the day the FBI ran up in here, but nobody blamed you. When you held that meeting last month, we assumed that it was bad, but we didn't know how bad. This is not your fault. I don't know one person in this building who has ever said one bad word about you," Jamal said. "Thank you so much Jamal."

"Let's hope everyone else feels the way you do. Well, let me get to it. Jamal you know if you ever need anything," "I'm good Job," Jamal interrupted. "I still work with the financial advisor you set me up with, and Kiara just got a promotion, so we are great." "That's great Jamal. Please tell her I said congratulations and I'm proud of both of you. You remind me a lot of Roni and me when we first started out." "I take that as a huge compliment," Jamal responded proudly. "How is the family by the way?" Job asked. Jamal looked away nervously. "Is everything okay Jamal?" "Yeah Job, everything is great." "What's that look about?" Job questioned.

"Umm, nothing I just…I mean," Jamal sighed heavily. "Kiara is pregnant." What?!?!" Job exclaimed. "Congratulations man…really," Job said as he hugged him. Jamal relaxed as he smiled proudly. He looked up to Job, and his opinion meant the world to him. "I'm sorry Job I didn't want to bring up any bad memories." "I understand Jamal, and I appreciate that, but you never have to worry about that. I'm truly happy for you both," Job smiled. "I am just so happy that I get another chance to do it right this time," Jamal smiled. "I am so blessed." "That you are Jamal, don't ever forget that. Please keep in touch with me and if you guys need anything at all seriously don't hesitate to give me a call." Thanks Job, "I appreciate it and you know I will," Jamal smiled hugging Job again.

As Job entered the elevator, he felt a sudden wave of sadness. He recalled the day Roni told him she was pregnant with Daniel. He did not think it was possible to love her more until she gave him the news. Job wiped away the tears as he exited the elevator. Job walked to his office and reviewed all the documents before him. He was going over his calculations for the third time when there was a knock on his door. Before he could say come in, the door opened.

"Hey Les, how are you?" Job asked. "I'm okay. How are you?" she asked. "I've had better days sis, but I'll get through it." "I hear you're having lunch with mom today," Leslie replied. "Yep, I'm heading over as soon as we wrap up things here." "Mom is so excited Job. I am so happy that you two are finally going to spend some time together," Leslie smiled. "I am too; I love her. "Nothing could ever change that. We had an interesting talk yesterday that I think was productive." "Good," Leslie said, "We need to stick together now more than ever." Job closed his eyes and nodded his head, "That's so true. Speaking of sticking together, Kim is going through a rough patch right now, and I invited her to stay with us for a while, and I was hoping that you would keep an eye on her for me.

Between us, she mentioned that there was some physical abuse going on with her soon-to-be ex-husband before she moved back and he showed up unexpectedly at her place last night." "Is she alright?" Leslie asked concerned. "Yes, but I think she's a bit shaken up. Also, would you mind staying too? I honestly I don't think it would look right otherwise." "Of course," Leslie said excitedly, "We can have a girl's night." Job shook his head. "Thank you so much, Leslie," Job said. "Well, it's about that time. You ready?" Leslie sighed. "Ready or not, I have to do this," Job said. Leslie hugged her brother.

Job and Leslie briefly met with his Matt, before heading to the conference room where everyone was waiting. "Are you sure this is what you want to do?" Matt asked for the last time. "Matt it's the only thing to do." Job hugged Leslie and took a deep breath before entering the conference room. Before he could speak, his entire staff stood to their feet and gave him a standing ovation.

Tears fell from Job's eyes. He was genuinely shocked at the gesture of love that he received from them. Job cleared his throat before speaking. "First off, I want to thank each one of you for your love, support, and prayers during this tough time for my family and me. I cannot begin to tell you how much your prayers, calls, food, cards, and flowers meant to us." "We love you Job," someone in the room yelled. Job smiled as his tears started flowing again.

"I love you all too," he continued. "The reason I called this meeting today is to fill you in on everything that has been happening and thank you all so much for your patience during this trying time for all of us. I know that this has not been easy on any of you.

First and foremost, I have been cleared of any wrongdoing by the FBI." "However," Job continued, "Samuel and the entire accounting department have essentially bankrupted the entire company." He heard the gasps around the room. "In addition to bankrupting the company, they depleted most of our retirement accounts." Job heard the murmuring all over the room.

He cleared his throat and continued. "I can't apologize enough to you for missing this. I hold myself accountable. The gentleman seated in the back is my lawyer. While I can't begin to make up for this deceit, I can at least ensure that you do not have to worry about paying your bills during this process.

My lawyer has $25,000 checks for each of you. I know that doesn't begin to repay what most of you are owed but trust me I won't rest until you all get every penny back that was stolen from you. Please contact Leslie with copies of your last 401K statements, and we'll begin the process of ensuring that your money is returned as timely as possible.

I ask for your patience because this will be a timely process, but in the meantime, if there is anything that I can do, please let me know. Again, I can't apologize to you enough, but I'm truly sorry." Job looked around the silent room. "Are there any questions?" He asked nervously. Jamal stood up first. "Job I want to thank you for thinking of us with everything else that you have to deal with right now. It's not your responsibility to do this, but that shows just the type of man that you are. Since the day I met you five years ago, I looked up to you and respected you. If it weren't for you, I know I would be dead or back in jail. I'm the husband and father that I am today because of your guidance and I appreciate everything you've done for me…for all of us."

Jamal fought to hold back tears, "Because of you, I've become a better man for my son, my family and myself." Job walked over and hugged Jamal tightly. Leslie wiped the tears from her eyes as Job looked over at her. He never expected this.

He thought that everyone would be angry with him or blame him. Job walked over to Matthew and embraced him. "Job I've never seen anyone with such favor." "To God be the glory," Job said. "You know three things we don't play with: our God, our momma, and our money and it's not always in that order," Matt laughed. "You are right about that." Job excused himself, noticing several of his staff members waiting to speak with him before receiving their checks.

Job received so many hugs and words of comfort. At one point, he looked up to the Heavens and thanked God for his grace and mercy. Job's staff loved him and was extremely devoted to him. Jamal was the last person to meet with him. "I don't know what to say about this Job," Jamal said. "I'm just trying to right the wrongs," Job said. Jamal started to tear up again. I have never met a more honorable man in my life. I meant it when I said I wanted to be like you."

"That's the God in me you see Jamal," Job smiled. "Strive to be like Him, and you will be fine. Things don't always turn out the way that you expect them to, but He has a plan. Trust me." Jamal hugged Job again before exiting the room. It had been a long day, and it's only 11:30.

"Well, I better get going. You know how mom hates it when we are late," Job said looking at his watch. "Yes, I do," Leslie said, remembering the time she came home 20 minutes late for dinner, and her mother made her eat sandwiches for a week while everyone else had delicious, hot home-cooked meals. Leslie handed her check back to Job.

"Job you just dished out more than three million dollars. I know you depleted most of your savings accounts do this. When you get back on your feet you can double it," she smiled. "I have more than enough stashed away." "I love you so much," Job said hugging her tightly. "I know you do, now go before mom has a fit," Leslie warned. "What are you going to do for the rest of the day?" Job asked. "Well I just sent Kim a text, and we're taking Anita to get Mani-pedis and having lunch afterward." "That's so sweet, I'll see you guys at home later," Job smiled before rushing off.

Job arrived at his childhood home with minutes to spare. He could smell the food as soon as he opened the door. Angela setting the table as Job entered the kitchen. "Perfect timing as always," she smiled. "You taught me well," Job said kissing her on the cheek. "It smells amazing in here," he said handing her a lovely bouquet of flowers.

[155]

"Thank you, baby," she said. Angela stood back to look at her son.

He looked so much like his father. Job knew what his mother thought as he hugged her tightly. "I miss him too mom." Angela fought back the tears and cleared her throat. Job washed his hands before sitting down at the table. He reached for her hand to say grace as she reached for a plate.

Angela looked at him hesitantly before accepting his hand. Job smiled as he began saying grace. Job was so happy to have this time with his mother. They hadn't talked like this in a long time. Angela and Job discussed the past, Roni and the children, his father, and his health.

Job tried his best to ease her fears. "Mom all I can do is pray," Job said rubbing her hand. "I believe that whatever happens will be His Will. If He allows me to continue living, He still has work for me to complete. If not, He wants me to be with my family. Either way mom, I'm okay with His decision."

"Would you still feel that way if Roni and the kids were here?" his mother asked. Job paused for a second to think about it, "I want to believe that I would be mother, but I honestly don't know. I wouldn't understand it, but I think I'd trust that God knows what's best and has a better plan for us." His mother begins crying. "Job, I want to trust in the Lord again, but I'm so afraid. Losing your father was the hardest thing that I've ever endured until this. I still remember the day I met him." Job smiled as his mother repeated the story that he'd heard so many times he could quote it verbatim.

"It was my first day at church when my family and I moved here from Atlanta. I was so nervous because I didn't know anyone. Your father offered me the seat next to him, and I was by his side from that day until the last day of his life. I can't lose you too," Angela cried. "I can't. That would be like losing your father all over again." "Mother you are not going to lose me. Even if I am not here with you physically, I will always be with you; just like dad is still with us. I feel his presence all the time," Job smiled.

"Job will you pray with me please?" his mother asked. Job had waited for this day for so long. "Mother I would love nothing more," he beamed. Job and his mother prayed together for the next hour. They were both so happy when they finished. "I know pop is up in Heaven two-steppin'," Job smiled as his mother laughed. "I bet he is too," Angela said, wiping her tears away. "Thank you, baby; I feel like a huge burden has been removed from my shoulders. I was so lost in my pain. I loved your father for almost as long as I have been alive, and I miss him. Job, I am so sorry for the way I've treated you. Please forgive me," his mother cried.

"Mother there is nothing to forgive. I understand, and I knew just like God knew that you would come back," Job smiled. "I'll tell you one thing," she said, "I'm going to pray like never before. I need you Job. If it's God's Will, then it's His will, but I'm going to pray until He says otherwise." "Me too mom," Job smiled, "Me too."

Job drove home on cloud nine listening to one of his favorite songs by *Marvin Sapp, 'Never Would Have Made It'*. Job was so happy that his mom had come back to herself. As he drove up in the driveway, he felt so good. Kim and Leslie were in the sunroom laughing like a couple of school girls when he entered the house. Job smiled at the sight and shook his head.

"Hey, when did you get back?" Leslie asked, noticing that he'd entered the room. "Just now," he said, "What are you two laughing about?" "Your high-top fade," Leslie laughed. Kim fell over on her side she was laughing so hard. "Y'all are crazy," Job smiled. "My fade was fresh to def." Leslie and Kim laughed even harder. Kim wiped her eyes as Job sat down beside Leslie.

"Job thank you so much," Kim said, wiping the tears from her eyes. "I appreciate this. I have not had a girl's day since college. We had so much fun." "I'm glad; it feels good to have some laughter in this house again," Job smiled. Leslie nodded her head in agreement. "So, are we still on for dinner and a movie tonight?" Job asked as Anita walked in with a bottle of water for Job. "We sure are," Anita said." "I can't wait." Job smiled as he stood to hug Anita. "I hear things went well today?" Anita smiled as she sat next to him. Job nodded as he swallowed the water. "Unbelievably well Anita," Job smiled. "We even prayed together," Job said beaming. "Wow, that is amazing," Leslie smiled. "I knew if anyone could do it, it'd be you." Job shook his head. "That wasn't me, that was all God," he smiled.

"I didn't even see that coming, but it feels so good to see some sunshine through the rain finally." Before he could continue the phone rang. Anita answered the phone while Kim and Leslie tried to decide on a movie. Job could tell from Anita's conversation that it was Matt on the phone. Job accepted the phone from Anita.

"So, Ashleigh's mother has retained a lawyer, and they want to settle out of court, "he said, hanging up the phone. "Are you serious?" Leslie asked. "This woman has a lot of nerve." "She's willing to settle for 10 million dollars." Kim started to choke on her tea, "My God she can't be serious." "She's very serious. She initially wanted 100

million." "Well that just shows you that her lawyers know this is a frivolous lawsuit," Leslie added. "Why would they go from 100 to 10? This lawsuit isn't about Ashleigh," Leslie said shaking her head, thinking about the sweet young lady. "You and Roni practically raised that girl. I can't believe the nerve of some people," Anita said.

Leslie walked over to her brother. "Job I know you're a good man, and you always want to do the right thing. I love that most about you." "I feel a but coming on," Job said. "But," Leslie continued, "You need to fight this Job. She is exploiting her daughter's death for financial gain." "I don't know," Job sighed as he rubbed his temples.

"A part of me feels as if she is only after money. Ashleigh spent so much time here I felt like she was one of my children. I understand that she was her mom's only child, but it hurts to think that she's just after money now. I don't want to believe in my heart that any mother could be that cold." The women all shook their heads. "Regrettably, there will always be opportunists who want to take advantage of situations like this. It's heartbreaking," Leslie said. "Ashleigh was such a sweetie pie." Anita smiled, thinking about the girl's bright, dimpled smile that lit up the room.

"Okay enough of the negativity," Job said. "This is our night out, and we're going to have fun. No tears. Agreed?" "Agreed," they all said. "Good. Now I'm going to go shower and change. Where are we going for dinner"? He asked. "I was thinking Del Frisco's," Kim said. "Yes, I love their calamari," Anita said. "Can't forget that Butter Cake," Leslie added. "Del Frisco's, it is," Job said. Great, I made the reservation for 6:00 that way we can still see an early movie," Kim says. "Perfect," Anita smiled. "I need to go make myself pretty."

As they drove to the restaurant, they listened to a radio station playing all the oldies but goodies from the 70's, singing along with the classics and enjoying themselves. They had a great time at dinner and the theater. As they rode home after the movie, they had so much fun laughing and talking about their outing. "I cannot remember the last time I've been to the movies," Anita said.

"Yes, that was so much fun," Leslie agreed, "Thank you so much Kim." "Yes, thank you Kim," Job said. "We should make this a regular thing," Kim said excitedly. "We should talk to mommy, Danielle, and Adrienne about starting a girl's night outing once a month," Leslie said. "That sounds like so much fun," Kim smiled. "It's settled then," Anita said.

"Hey, what about me?" Job pouted. "You guys should get together and have a boy's night," Leslie suggested. "That is a great idea," Job agreed. He and his brothers had not spent any time together since a few years before his father passed away. Job sat back staring out the window. He didn't know what the future held for him and decided that he did not want to waste any time wishing he had spent more time with his family. Job pulled out his phone and texted Marcus to help him make plans for a boy's night out.

# CHAPTER TWENTY

# ONE YEAR LATER

"Okay Mack, you sounded a little funny on the phone. What's up?" Job asked. "I don't know how to tell you this," Mack said. "Just tell me," Job said. "Job the tumor is gone. I mean completely gone. When we did the CT scan last week, I didn't see anything; which is why I had you come back for another one on Monday. I also had several of my colleagues' review them, and none of us can find any trace of a tumor. I can't explain it." Job started laughing hysterically. "Job, are you okay?" Mack asked nervously. "Okay? Mack, I'm more than okay!" Job said. "Thank you Jesus!" "I just don't get it," Mack said.

"The favor of God cannot be explained or contained Mack." "It just is what it is," Job laughed as he continued praising God. "What are you and Keisha doing tonight?" Job asked. "We don't have any plans," Mack said. "Great I want you both to have dinner with my family tonight," Job said hugging his longtime friend. "That sounds good; we had a ball at the last BBQ, thank you for the invite," Mack smiled.

Job called Anita from the car and told her that he wanted to take the entire family out for dinner and asked her to call them and make the arrangements. Anita reserved a private room for dinner. As they finished their meal, Job tapped his glass as he stood to address his family. "I want to thank you all for coming," Job said as looked around at his entire family including Kim and Leslie's fiancé Michael sitting around the dinner table.

Everyone at the table was on pins and needles. The last time Job had invited everyone to get together; he'd given them the devastating news about his diagnosis. "Let me just start by saying that we serve an awesome God." "Yes, we do," everyone at the table agreed. "This has been one heck of a year, but because of every one of you, I made it, and I'm stronger than ever. I gathered you all here tonight to inform you that I had another CT scan, and there is not a single trace of a tumor anywhere. Also, Samuel had a change of heart, not only did he return every penny that he stole but he came back to face the charges, and since the investigators have confirmed that I was not involved with any of it, J.A. Investments will be back in business starting next Monday." "Thank God!" Anita exclaimed.

Everyone rushed to hug Job. "Job next time talk a little faster," Carlos said relieved, "You had my heart in my stomach. I love you, man." "I love you too," Job smiled. "Thank you God for keeping my son safe," Angela prayed as she hugged Job. She was a completely changed woman since she and Job had lunch one year ago. Angela was more devoted and faithful now than she had ever been in her life. She had started attending church again and she, Anita and a few of the other mothers of the church participated in several outreach programs in the community.

Kim walked over and timidly hugged Job with tears brimming in her eyes. "Job I am so happy for you," she smiled. "Thank you, Kim," Job said as he reached out to wipe away the tears that fell from her eyes gently. Everyone at the table noticed the simple gesture that spoke volumes.

Anita smiled as she and Angela clasped hands hoping that the two would end up together. They had been watching the love blossoming between them for the last six months even though both fought to ignore it. Everyone continued to have a wonderful time at dinner, and anyone at the table did not miss the stolen glances between Job and Kim. Job, Kim, and Anita arrived home shortly before midnight.

"Well I have to be up early," Anita said. I'll see you two in the morning." Kim hugged Anita. They had become quite close in the last year. After they say their good nights, Anita walked over to Job and hugged him once again. "God is so good," Anita smiled. "Goodnight love," Job smiled kissing Anita on the cheek. "Goodnight baby," she said as she headed to her room.

Job sat quietly across from Kim in the living room, noticing that she was avoiding eye contact. He had so much to say but didn't know where to begin. "Well, I guess I'll turn in too, goodnight Job and congratulations again," she smiled. "I'd like to talk to you about something if you're not too tired," Job said anxiously. "Sure, is everything okay?" Kim asked. "Everything is perfect," Job said. "I'm not sure where to start," he smiled nervously. "The beginning is always a good place," she smiled. "Okay, smarty-pants" Job laughed, clearing his throat.

"I thought your timing for reappearing in my life was a little odd, but I never questioned it or God." I just went with the flow. Kim nodded. "I think He brought you back to be my wife," Job said, trying to gage Kim's reaction. Over the last year, she had fallen so deeply in love with Job all over again, but she felt guilty. "I know it's a bit sudden, but you have always held a special place in my heart Kimmy. I'll always love my wife and children, but I feel that God is giving me a second chance, giving us a second chance."

"Job, I care about you so much. I would be lying if I said that those were not the words that I have been praying to hear but I must admit that I have also been struggling with a lot of guilt. Why would you feel guilty?" Job asked as he sat beside her, wiping her tears. "Job this is the home you shared with your wife and children, and here I am living in her home, falling in love with you again." "You say that like it's a bad thing." "Job it's not that," Kim sighed, "I just don't feel that it is appropriate." "I understand what you mean, and I've struggled with that as well," Job said. "Wondering what people would think or say, but I've prayed about this for a while, and I believe that you're meant to be my wife." "I just don't want people judging either of us Job," Kim cried. "Kimmy this is about us, no one else." "I don't care what anyone one thinks."

"Look, I know this is a lot to take in all at once, so I understand if you want to think about it for a while. We can take things as slow as you want. All I ask is that you think about it okay?" Job asked. Kim held her head down as the tears fell. "Job it's not just that. I do love you, but there is something that I've never told you.

As you know, I've had several miscarriages, and all the doctors and specialists say I will never be able to have children." Kim closed her eyes. "Job I know how much you love children and I could never, ever take that from you," Kim cried. "Kim, I'd love to have more children someday, but if we can't, we'll adopt.

The only thing I am sure of is my love for you." "Look it's been a long day," Job said. "I guess we'd better turn in. See you at 5:30?" Job asked. "Yes," Kim said quietly. Kim and Job had been jogging together every morning for the last four months. Kim's life has changed so much. With the help of Job's team of lawyers, she was finally able to get Gerald out of her life once and for all. Her divorce was finally complete.

As Kim walked to her room she thought about everything Job had said. Kim was happier than she had been in a very long time, but she was also terrified. She knew that Job would always love his wife and she didn't have an issue with that. She was more concerned with having such huge footsteps to follow.

Kim tossed and turned for several hours before finally drifting off to sleep. Kim dreamt of a presence in her room. As she looked up, she saw Roni. "Hello Kim," Roni smiled. "I'm sorry we didn't get to meet under different circumstances." "Me too," Kim said with a touch of sadness in her voice. "I'm so sorry Roni; I never meant for any of this to happen."

"Sorry for what?" Roni asked. Kim began to cry. "I'm living in your home, and I should not have the feelings that I feel for Job." "Why not, Job is an amazing man, and I need you to take care of him for me," she said. "He needs you just as much as you need him. I am happy that he has you in his life." "Roni, I could never compare to you," Kim said as tears continue to flow.

"There is no comparison Kim. Job loves us both in unique special ways. He loves you Kim, and anyone can see that you love him too. God has given you both a second chance at love and happiness, and you deserve it Kim. I could not have picked a better woman for him," Roni smiled as she walked away.

Kim opened her eyes as the tears continue to fall down her cheeks. Her dream was just the validation that she needed. As Kim got up and dressed for her run with Job, she felt like a huge burden had been lifted from her shoulders. Job was in the kitchen stretching when she arrived. "Good morning," Kim said. "Good Morning," he smiled. "You are glowing", Job said. "I slept great last night," Kim responded. "Great, I'm glad," Job smiled. "You ready?" "I am," Kim said softly. Job felt like he was 15 all over again. "Do you mind if we walk the rest of the way?" Kim asked 30 minutes into their run. "I'd like to talk to you about something." "Sure, what's on your mind?" Job asked, looking at her as he slowed his pace to a stop.

"Job this is going to sound crazy I know, but last night I had a dream about Roni," she said. "That doesn't sound crazy at all," Job said, catching his breath. "In the dream, she said it was okay for me to love you and asked me to take care of you. It was so real," Kim said. "I can't explain it but it's like I felt her presence. Kim could still remember the dream so vividly. Are you okay?" Job asked. "I don't know, it's just," Kim rambled, trying to find the right words to express her feelings. "Kim, God works in mysterious ways.

Look at the paths our lives took to lead us back to this moment." "If I am honest with myself, I've always loved you," Job said. "I wasn't sure how to process my feelings at first. I felt guilty months after losing Roni and the kids, but I realized that my love for you doesn't diminish the love I have for Roni. You're my first love. So where do we go from here?" Job asked.

"I am not quite sure," Kim said. "I guess we should just pray and go with the flow," she smiled at Job as she tossed the words he had previously spoken back at him. "Okay, so you're using my words back on me now," Job laughed. "How about dinner tonight?" he asked. "Sure, I would love that," Kim said. "Perfect, so it's a date?" Job asked nervously.

"Yes, it's a date," Kim smiled. "Good," Job sighed deeply. "Now the last one to the house is a rotten egg," Job said as he took off with Kim following closely behind him. As they ran up to the house, he beat her by a quarter of an inch. "I want a rematch," Kim laughed. "I want my breakfast," Job said. "You will get your breakfast you little cheater," Kim laughed as she lightly pushed him.

"What's on your agenda for the day?" Job asked. "I have to tie up a few loose ends on an old case, so it should be a pretty light day today," Kim said. "Great!" Job said. "You think you can get off a little early?" "That shouldn't be a problem," Kim said as she looked at him curiously while he smirked.

"What are you up to Jobias Arrington?" Kim asked. "That's for me to know my dear and you to find out," Job teased. "Have you forgotten that I am a renowned investigator?" Kim asked. Job continued to laugh. "Well I am heading to the office for a while to get things ready for Monday," Job said excitedly. "I am so happy for you," Kim said. "Me too," Job said, "I feel like this is a season of restoration for me.

I'm thrilled that I can finally call my staff back to work. This year has been hard on us all, but I have learned some valuable lessons in the process." "And that is most important," Kim said. "Yep. Well, let me get ready. It's going to be a long day." "You need any help?" Kim asked. "No babes I'm good, but thank you," Job said. Kim blushed. "What?" he asked. "It's just been a while since you've called me that. It feels nice," Kim smiled. "I'm glad," Job said.

He hesitated slightly before walking over to her, grasping her hand and kissing her softly on her lips. "I've wanted to do that for a long time," Job said nervously. "Me too," Kim said blushing again. Anita walked in and cleared her throat. "Good morning Anita," they both said as they jumped apart, smiling like two teenagers in love. Anita was so happy for them. "Well, I have to shower and get dressed. I'll see you in a little while," Job said slowly releasing her hand. "Okay," Kim said softly.

Anita turned her back to give them a little privacy. "Anita I'm going to shower. I can come back to help if you want," Kim said. "Okay baby, that would be nice," Anita said. Anita didn't need any help, but she had a feeling that Kim wanted to talk to her. Thirty minutes later, Kim returned to the kitchen refreshed from her shower. "So, what do you think banana walnut waffles?" Anita asked "Yes," Kim said excitedly, "Can you please teach me how to make them?" "I'd love to," Anita said. "They are Job's favorite." Kim was determined to make that they were perfect.

"Thank you so much for teaching me Anita; you are such a fantastic cook. My mom wasn't much of a cook, but she could bake like nobody's business. I have always wanted to learn how to cook." "Well you came to the right place," Anita smiled, handing Kim an apron. As Anita ran off the list of items for Kim to retrieve from the fridge, Kim became very quiet. "You okay baby? Something on your mind?" Anita asked. Kim wasn't sure how to respond. Anita turned Kim around to face her, "You love him, and he loves you," Anita smiled.

"That's all that matters," Anita said. "How did you know?" Kim asked. "Girl, Stevie Wonder could see the sparks flying between you two," Anita laughed. "Last night

I had a dream about Roni, and in the dream, she asked me to take care of Job."

"Anita, I feel so guilty, Kim complained" "What do you have to feel guilty about?" Anita asked. "I have lived in this woman's house for a year and now." Anita stopped her, "Baby as hard as it is to hear it, this was all part of God's plan. God knew all this would happen. Things were supposed to happen this way," Anita said hugging Kim. "People will probably think I was planning this all along," Kim cried. "Baby people will always think and talk. You can't focus on people. Do you love him?" Anita asked. Kim couldn't suppress her smile. "Yes, I do Anita," Kim said.

"Good," Anita responded because Job loves you too and that's what matters." "Okay," Kim sighed, "Are you okay with all of this?" Kim asked Anita. "I couldn't be more okay with it," Anita smiled and hugged Kim, "I love you both so much and want you to be happy. I couldn't have chosen a better woman for him." "Anita those were Roni's exact words in the dream." Anita smiled and hugged her tightly. "See everything is going to be just fine. You have to trust God and stop worrying about that other people will think. God says He will make our latter greater than our former and he's proving His word now."

Job returned a short while later and was truly impressed when Anita told him that Kim fixed breakfast. "Kim, this is amazing," Job said as he devoured his food. "Thank you," Kim said proudly, watching as he continued to inhale his food. Job looked up and caught her watching him before she turned away blushing. He was determined to show her the type of love that she had never known.

After breakfast, Job asked Kim to walk him to the car. Job kissed her once again. Kim felts as if she was going to faint. "I'm going to miss you," Job said. "Me too," Kim smiled shyly. "I don't know how I am going to get any work done," Job smiled. "I feel like I'm 15 all over again," he laughed. "Who would've known we'd end up here," Kim said shaking her head.

"God knew," Job smiled and grasped her hands. Job prayed a prayer of protection over Kim as he held her hands. She had never felt as loved than she did right then at that moment. "Well, let me go," Job said. "I could stand here and stare into your eyes forever." Kim blushed once again. "Drive safely," she said. "You too babe," Job smiled. "See you soon." Job had a long day ahead of him and only had a few hours to make it work. He planned to propose to Kim tonight.

He wanted to make it special for her. She'd been through so much, and he wanted to make sure that it was something she'd remember forever. Job finished up things at work sooner than he expected. His focus was now on Kim, and he wanted to make sure everything was perfect. He contacted Anita, his sisters and her friends to make sure he had not forgotten anything. When Kim walked out of her building, she noticed Sean waiting for her. "Hi, Sean. What are you doing here?" she asked nervously, thinking that something had happened to Job. "Job asked me to give you this," he smiled. Kim reads the note from Job.

*Hi babe-Sean will drive you home. (Wow I love the sound of that, home) I have a few surprises waiting for you. I hope you like them. See you soon love. J*

Kim was grinning from ear to ear as Sean opened the car door for her. Inside the car was a beautiful bouquet of calla lilies. Kim leaned back and enjoyed her pampering. Her ex-husband wasn't romantic at all. She knew that she was going to be in for a treat dating Job. As the car pulled up to the house, Anita greeted Kim at the door. "Well I don't think I have ever seen you smile so hard before," Anita teased.

"Job is the sweetest. He…" Before Kim could finish her statement, she looked around the house, and there were flowers everywhere. Kim's mouth dropped open. She looked at Anita who laughed. "Well, they aren't for me." Kim could not believe her eyes. As she turned the corner, she saw one of her closest friends and hair stylist sitting on the sofa.

"Jasmine, girl what are you doing here?" Kim asked. "I'm here to do your hair and Pam is here to do your nails." Kim looked over at Pam who was preparing her tools. "But "how…?" Kim asked. Before she finished her question, she answered her own question. "Job," She, Jasmine and Pam said at the same time.

"Girl you've got a keeper right there," Jasmine smiled. "He paid me enough to cover all of my clients for today and then some. He's a nice guy. I'm so happy for you," Jasmine said as she hugged her friend. "Thank you, Jasmine," Kim smiled. "Alright now let's get to it because I am on a deadline," Jasmine said as she pushed Kim toward her bedroom. "Alright, alright," Kim laughed.

Kim felt so giddy. She'd never been spoiled like this before. Kim went to her room to shower and wash her hair. When she walked in, she noticed a beautiful dress on the bed with a pair of matching shoes, complete with accessories.

Kim couldn't believe her eyes. When Job said he had some surprises, he was not kidding. As she opened the bathroom door, the floor was covered with rose petals, and the tub filled with bubbles. There was another card on the counter from Job she guessed.

*I hope you are enjoying your surprises. I can't wait to see you later…counting the seconds. I love you baby. J*

Kim held the card to her heart. She was overwhelmed with emotion at the thought of all the planning Job must've done to set this up. She couldn't believe that he did all of this for her. Kim was enjoying her nice relaxing bubble bath when Anita knocked at her door.

"Hey baby, when you're done, Job has another surprise waiting for you," Anita said through the door. "Anita, I feel like I am dreaming," Kim said through tears. Anita opened the door and smiled, "It's all real baby. You enjoy it. You both deserve it.

Here's a robe for you, someone is waiting for you in the other room." "Thank you, Anita," Kim said. Anita smiled, closing the door. When Kim exited the bathroom, she noticed a massage table set up on the balcony. As she walked over, a young lady was waiting for her.

"Hello, Kim. My name is Karyn. I'll be your masseuse." Kim smiled. "Let me guess, Job sent you." Karyn laughs. "That's quite a man you have there." "Yes, he is," Kim smiled back. "I am so blessed." "Okay, when you're comfortable, please lie down on the table," Karyn said. "Do you prefer Swedish or deep tissue? She asked. "I have never had a massage," Kim said. "Oh well you are in for quite a treat," Karyn smiled as she helped Kim onto the table.

Kim laid on the table and closed her eyes as Karyn began to work her magic. Kim felt like she was in Heaven. "I can't believe that I've been missing this all of my life," Kim moaned.

An hour later Kim felt more relaxed than she had felt in a very long time. She exited the room with a huge smile on her face. Kim couldn't believe that Job had put so much thought into this date. She silently thanked God for her second chance at loving him.

"Wow!" Jasmine said as she saw the smile on Kim's face, "Someone is in love." "Jasmine, I honestly think I am," Kim responded. "It scares me so much."

"Why?" Jasmine asked. "What if this is all too soon for both of us? Or what if Job realizes that this is all moving too fast for him and decides that he's not ready for this?" "Losing him again would destroy me," Kim cried. "Pam, would you excuse us for a moment please?" Jasmine asked. "Of course," Pam said.

Jasmine sat next to Kim. "Sweetie, don't even let the enemy get into your head. God created that man for you. I believe that all of this is a part of His plan." "I want to believe that too Jasmine, but things like this don't happen for me. Gerald broke me down mentally and physically for so long. I don't feel worthy of a man like Job. I can't even give him children."

"Girl, that was the enemy using Gerald," Jasmine said. "You are more than worthy of a man like Job. He has been to hell and back, and you have stood by his side the entire time. You are an amazing woman Kim. You don't give yourself enough credit sometimes. I have never told anyone this, but when I met Eddie, I had been through so much with my ex-boyfriend that I promised myself that I would never, ever date another man."

"I met a woman who treated me like a queen, but I felt so guilty because growing up I heard that God hates sinners and I was raised to believe that homosexuality was a sin. I thought God hated me. Girl let me tell you that was a lie from the pit of hell. I was conflicted, and I felt so alone. I didn't want to live anymore." Kim couldn't believe her ears. "Jasmine I had no idea" Kim cried. "No one knew," Jasmine whispered. "My parents were pastors and completely disowned me. I was working for FedEx back then, and I was assigned to train Eddie when he started working with the company. We got along great. He told me right away that he was a pastor."

"I felt like God was trying to tell me something. I grew up in church and even during everything going on in my life I never stopped loving God, even though there were many times I wondered if He still loved me."

"Eddie and I would talk about God often, and one day I'd had enough and decided that I no longer wanted to live the life that I was living, but I didn't feel as if I had much of an option for a way out."

"By this time, I was convinced that I would be alone for the rest of my life. I fell into such a deep depression that I didn't want to live anymore. I had not shown up for work for about three days straight which is out of character for me, but I was so depressed that I could not even get out of bed. I wasn't answering my phone or anything. On that 4th day; it was a Friday, Eddie showed up at my house and banged on my door for what felt like hours."

"Finally, he said if I didn't open the door he'd knock it down to make sure I was okay, and I knew he would. For two hours, we just sat there in silence and then he said something that made me cry like a baby. He said God told me to tell you that He loves you unconditionally and he wants you to stop running."

"Girl I bawled like a newborn baby. We talked all night long. I mean literally until the sun came up. We prayed together that night, and I rededicated my life back to God. I went to church with him that Sunday and officially gave my life back to the Lord and it was like someone flipped a switch. I won't lie; initially, I still had my struggles, but like the Bible says, resist the devil, and he will flee. Once the enemy realized that I wasn't going back, the temptation was gone. I was even starting to have visions of being married with kids."

"A couple of years later Eddie asked me out. I said yes, and here we are ten years and counting. We all deserve love Kim. We are all worthy of love," Jasmine said hugging Kim. "Thank you so much Jasmine, and thank you for sharing that with me," Kim cried. "Anytime girl, tell the truth and shame the devil. Now let's get you ready before Job thinks you've changed your mind." Kim sat back and smiles and whispered, "I do deserve this."

Two hours later Kim was staring at herself in the mirror. The dress that Job picked out for her fit her like a glove. Jasmine and Anita could not stop the tears flowing down their faces. Kim hugged Anita and Jasmine tightly before heading out for her date with Job. Kim closed her eyes and thanked God for sending him back to her as she entered the waiting limo. Kim was in her own world as the car pulled to a stop.

When the door opened, she stepped out and looked into the eyes of the man that had stolen her heart since she was 14 years old. Kim flung her arms around Job as he stared at her with his mouth open. "You like?" Kim asked with a huge grin. "I love!" Job responded when he finally found his voice. "You look beautiful," Job beamed. People turned to watch as Job and Kim walk down the pier to the yacht. They made a very stunning couple. Their captain, Andrew, was waiting to help Kim and Job board. "Kim, Job welcome aboard," he smiled. "Right this way. Job everything is ready, just as you requested". "Thanks Drew," Job responded.

Kim looked around as the crew began to set sail. She had never been on a yacht before. "Job this is amazing, is this yours?" Kim asked. "Yes," Job smiled. The sun was beginning to set in the distance, and the sky filled with beautiful hues of purple, pink and orange. "I love the water. I have never seen anything so beautiful," Kim said as she watched the sunset.

"Neither have I," Job said watching her. Kim blushed as she turned to look at him. "Job this has been the best day of my life. I don't know where to begin. This day has been like a fairytale. Thank you so much for everything. I love you so much," Kim said as she fought to stop the tears that threatened to fall. Job closed his eyes the moment words fell from her lips. "I love you too Kim. I am so in love with you that it makes my heart hurt," Job said with tears in his eyes.

Kim could no longer control her tears. "I knew I was in love with you months ago," Job continues. "I initially struggled with some guilt too, but I asked God to remove it if this was His will for my life and He did it." "I have never been so happy," Kim said as she allowed the tears to flow. "This happened so fast and unexpectedly, but I do love you, more than I ever imagined that I could." Job kissed her softly before leading her to the deck. There was a table set beautifully with her favorite foods. Kim could not believe her eyes. "Job," Kim gushed. "I cannot believe you."

After dinner, Job took her hand. "Kim, I love you more than I can express to you. When we parted after graduation, I was so hurt, but I knew you'd return to me. I knew from the day I met you at Mack's birthday party, that you were meant to be my wife. I hope you don't think I'm moving too fast but," he said as he dropped to his knee.

"I love you, Kimmy. God brought you back to me during one of the most difficult seasons of my life, and from those ashes, our love was rekindled. Kimberly Camille Godwin, will you please do me the honor of allowing me to love you each and every second of every day for the remainder of my life? Will you trust me with the precious gift of your heart and allow me to be your Boaz and love you with the love of Christ? Will you be my wife?" "Yes, yes, yes!" Kim cried.

# Six Months Later

Job and Kim boarded the yacht again to celebrate the anniversary of their six-month engagement. After dinner, they noticed a small beach with a beautiful white tent. Job suggested that they take a closer look at the breathtaking sight. "Are you sure?" Kim asked. "Sure, why not?" Job asked. There were candles and flowers everywhere. "Wow, this is beautiful," Kim smiled.

"Yes, it is," Job commented. As they exited the boat, they both took off their shoes to walk along the sand. They could hear music playing, as they got closer to the tent. "Job maybe we shouldn't," Kim said suddenly apprehensive. "Let's just creep in the back and take a quick look," Job suggested.

As they entered the tent, everyone stood and turned toward them. Kim was just about to turn around to leave until she saw Jasmine and Leslie standing at the front of the tent with all of Job's brothers. As Kim continued looking around, she noticed several of her co-workers including Agent Williamson and his wife, along with Anita and Angela.

Kim turned to ask Job what was going on when she saw him down on one knee smiling. "Kimberly Camille Godwin, I love you and don't want one more day to go by without being your husband. I don't know what I would've done without you by my side this past year and a half. You have been my best friend and my confidant. I kneel here tonight before God, you and all our family and friends asking you to grant me the pleasure of loving you for the rest of my life starting tonight. Will you marry me right now?" Kim began crying as she nodded yes.

As soon as Kim said yes; *Chrisette Michelle's, 'Golden'* began playing. Job held Kim's hand as they walked together down the aisle. As they reached the front, they turned and faced each other. Kim realized that she wasn't the only one crying as tears fell from Job's eyes. She wiped his tears from his cheek as he softly kissed her hand. Minutes later Job and Kim were officially husband and wife.

Job softly kissed her as she held him tightly. As they exited the tent, there was a large reception area that neither of them noticed on the way inside. They prepared for their first dance as husband and wife, walking to the center of the makeshift dance-floor when their favorite song from high school began to play. Job used to sing *The*

*Deele's, Two Occasions* to Kim every night before they hung up the phone when they were younger. Job smiled as Kim started to cry as she reminisced. Job began singing to Kim along with the lyrics. "Cause every time I close my eyes I think of you…" Kim smiled as she looked into the eyes of her husband.

## Eight Months Later | New Beginnings

"Kim, if you don't sit yourself down somewhere," Jasmine fussed. "You know if Job comes in here and sees you doing anything he's going to go off and I will not be getting the blame." "I can't help it," Kim laughed. "I feel so bad; sitting here while you guys work." "Trust me with those three in your belly you will have more than enough to do in no time," Jasmine said.

"I'm sure," Kim smiled rubbing her large belly. "I can't believe I'm going to be a mommy," Kim cried. "Kim you're going to make me cry," Leslie said. "Okay, let's all stop this now before I'm somewhere sobbing and snotting," Jasmine laughed trying to lighten the mood. "I love what you did with the house Kim," Pam commented as she looked around. "Thanks," Kim smiled, "Job worked so hard to finish the house before the babies arrived."

"Well it has paid off," Leslie said, "It's beautiful." "Thank you," Kim said softly. "I still have to pinch myself sometimes because I cannot believe that this is my life. What a difference a year makes," Kim smiled. "You're telling me," Leslie laughed. "This time last year, we were both single, and now we're married with children on the way." "I'm so happy that our babies are going to grow up together," Kim says, "I've always wanted a big family." "Well you will have that and then some," Pam laughed.

Angela and Anita walked in carrying big platters of sandwiches. Leslie and Kim made a beeline for the table as soon as they spotted the food. "You two are going to eat up the food before the guests arrive," Anita laughed. "We can't help it, between the two of us, we're eating for seven," Leslie said, grabbing two sandwiches. "Lord help us all," Anita laughed. "I can't wait to spoil these babies," Angela smiled. Me too," they all said together and started laughing again. Job and Michael walked in carrying a ton of gifts. "Hey what's this about?" Job asked.

Kim looked adoringly at her husband. "We were just saying how much we can't wait to spoil the little ones," Kim said. "How are daddy's babies?" Job asked as he knelt and kissed his wife's belly. The babies started moving at the sound of Job's voice. "They love their daddy," Kim smiled. "And their daddy loves them and their mommy," Job smiled. As Kim's baby shower got underway, Job looked at his wife sitting next to him. Job had never seen her look more beautiful. He gazed around at his family and friends playing games and laughing and felt such indescribable joy.

*"Lord I thank you that my cup runneth over"* Job prayed. *"I am so humbled by your grace and mercy. Thank you for loving me and blessing me. I will continue to serve you all the days of my life."*

The End

# Dedicated to the loving memories of:

Alexander & Elester Washington

Apostle Albert Venson, Sr

Louis Ridley, Jr

Louis Ridley, Sr

Mary E. Washington

Rachelle C. Evans

Will F. Morris

# One Last Thing…

I hope that you've enjoyed reading Job as much as I enjoyed writing it. This has truly been a labor of love and I thank you all for your support.

Finally, I'd like to ask you for a favor. If you've enjoyed reading this book, please be kind enough to leave a review on Amazon. I'd greatly appreciate it!

Click here to leave a review for this book on Amazon!

LSW

## Coming Soon

### Sins of a Father

### The Prodigal Sons

www.ingramcontent.com/pod-product-compliance
Lightning Source LLC
Chambersburg PA
CBHW070021260626
47159CB00005B/1899